Bleeding LOVE

A Hope Town novel

HARPER SLOAN

Cover Design by Sommer Stein with Perfect Pear Creative Covers
Cover Photography by Perrywinkle Photography
Editing by Ellie with Lovenbooks.com and Emma Mack
Cover Models : BT Urruela and Laura Chwat
Formatting by Champagne Formats

To Contact Harper:

Email: Authorharpersloan@gmail.com
Website: www.authorharpersloan.com
Facebook: www.facebook.com/harpersloanbooks

Other Books by Harper Sloan:

Corps Security Series:
Axel
Cage
Beck
Uncaged
Cooper
Locke

Hope Town Series:
Unexpected Fate

Disclaimer:

This book is not suitable for younger readers. There is strong
language, and adult situations.

Bleeding LOVE Playlist

Speakers by Sam Hunt

Bright by Echosmith

Dead in the Water by Ellie Goulding

Nothing Left to Lose by Kari Kimmel

Jealous by Labrinth

Love Me Like You Do by Ellie Goulding

Get Me Some of That by Thomas Rhett

Home to Mama by Justin Bieber

Make You Miss Me by Sam Hunt

Brown Eyed Girl by Van Morrison

Human by Jon McLaughlin

Photograph by Ed Sheeran

Everything by Lifehouse

Must Be Doin' Somethin' Right by Billy Currington

Marry Me by Train

I Choose You by Sara Bareilles

Silent Shouts by Adna

Hold My Hand by Jess Glynne

Capri by Cobie Caillat

Like I'm Gonna Lose You by Meghan Trainor

A Thousand Years by Christina Perri

To follow the Bleeding Love playlist, https://open.spotify.com/
user/1293550968/playlist/2dLpvRylcnJS4fX522BTQY

Dedication

To everyone who has ever needed a helping

hand and those still searching for theirs.

Never give up.

And know, you are never alone.

Even when you think that 'next step' is the

hardest one to take—

it's often the most beautiful.

Just . . . take my hand.

-Liam Beckett

A woman who opens her heart to love you, when it's already broken, is braver than any person you'll meet.
-Steven Benson

Prologue

Megan

HOLY SHIT.

What am I doing?

"Oh, God! Right there . . . I'm coming . . . Don't stop!"

Is that me screaming like that?

Holy shit.

I didn't even know that noises like that could come out of my mouth!

"You like that?" he asks with his lips pressed against my neck—the vibrations shooting straight to my core.

I focus, my now alcohol free vision, on the man thrusting above me. His dark hair is blending in with the shadows that are dancing around the room. His face is a mask of ecstasy as he thrusts into my waiting body. It's a look of pure desire that I will never forget.

What the hell am I doing?

"You feel so good. Your body so greedy for my cock. You want it harder, darlin'?"

I moan shamelessly and feel my body get even wetter with his huskily whispered words.

Screw it—this feels way too good to stop now.

I reach down, dig my fingers in the firm globes of his ass, tip my head back and beg. Beg with incoherent cries for him to take me harder. To take everything he can.

Two Hours Earlier

"You look beauuuutiful," I sing as Dani Reid—No, Dani Cage—walks over to sit next to me at one of the tables scattered around the backyard wedding.

She looks at me, her stunning green eyes bright with love and happiness.

"And you sound a little drunk, my friend," she laughs.

I just smile at her, running my fingers through the lace on her wedding gown. "This is soft."

She just laughs and leans back and looks across the yard to where her new husband, Cohen, is standing by the dock talking to some of his friends. This is another one of those moments when I'm reminded that this group doesn't have a single unattractive person in it. I take a second to look at all the well-built, good-looking men standing around him. When my eyes meet Liam Beckett's, I look away quickly. For months now Liam has made no secret that he would love nothing more than my undivided attention.

"They're all so unfairly hot. No men should be *that* attractive," I whisper in awe, gaining me another chuckle from Dani. I blush when I realize that my thoughts aren't staying in my head, where they belong. When I look back over to where the group of men are standing, my eyes hit the familiar pair of deep brown ones again, eyes that always seem to know each and every time I'm looking their way. I quickly look away, feeling that blush get even brighter. I'm not ready to deal with *him* right now. At least not when I'm this tipsy.

Picking up my wine glass, I take another healthy swallow as I do a quick scan, taking in all that is the Reid Family property. They've done a beautiful job transforming the backyard of Dani's family home for Cohen and Dani's wedding. I still can't believe that Dani managed to pull off a surprise wedding without Cohen even catching the smallest hint of her plans.

"Are you sure you're okay with Molly spending the night with my parents, Megs? I know it's hard for you to leave her overnight, but they just love your daughter to pieces. And I know Owen loves having her around." Dani reaches out and takes the hand I had resting against the table while she speaks.

"Yup," I smack and nod my head.

"You're drunk," she says, repeating her earlier observation.

"I'm not drunk, I'm tipsy. There's a huge difference there. If I was drunk I wouldn't be able to walk. Watch!"

I jump up from my chair with a little more power than I mean and quickly stumble when the narrow heel of my five-inch shoes sinks into the soft grass beneath me.

"Whoa, there darlin'."

I feel it, those words, every single syllable deep down in my gut. Each rumbled word vibrating through my body creating a slow burn until they end with a sharp pulse between my legs. His arms locked at my elbows and my back solidly against his front—where my graceless stumble caused me to end up. I jerk my body tight and feel his laughter reverberate through my body once again.

I attempt to pull my arms from his loose but strong hold, only to give up when it becomes clear that he isn't going to let go. Shifting until my face is turned, he lets one arm go and helps me spin until I'm facing him, and moves his hands from my elbows to my hips.

"Hey," he says with a smile, the dimple in his cheek popping out.

"Liam," I sigh and then curse myself for not being able to hide my reaction to him.

His smile turns knowing and his eyes darken before dropping to my lips.

I gulp.

"You should be more careful, Megs."

"It's Megan," I snap.

"I know, babe, you don't have to keep reminding me."

"Then why can't you seem to actually remember it?" I squeak and try to pull my body away from his grip—and fail, again.

"Someone doesn't sound *drunk* anymore." I hear Dani speak but I don't take my gaze off Liam. "She does look it though." She muses on a laugh, which finally gets my eyes to snap to hers.

"I'm fine! I just had a few glasses of wine and I haven't eaten much. But, I most definitely am not drunk. I think I would know if I was drunk."

Okay, so that's a lie. I might not be drunk, but I am definitely slightly past tipsy. Dealing with Liam—or rather my attraction to Liam—is hard enough for me on a good day, when I'm completely sober. But with this amount of wine flowing through my body, I just can't trust myself.

It's taken everything I have to keep him, and his obvious interest, at bay for the last couple months. When he's around he goes out of his way to get me alone and lay it out. He wants me.

"You look stunning when those shadows aren't rolling around your shoulders," Liam whispers, his lips press close enough to my ear that I can feel his words one by one against my skin.

I shiver, his words hitting me close to home, but the tone causing me to forget I should be pushing him away. Especially when he's talking about things that he has no business speaking about.

"I'm fine," I stammer.

"Yeah, darlin', I know you are."

His eyes keep their hypnotizing hold on my own. I hear Dani excuse herself. I don't turn to watch her disappear in the lingering crowd of party-goers that are still left milling around. The music is still floating in the air around us. As I look into his eyes everything around me feels like it's . . . alive. It's a feeling that I've been missing for the last few years. A feeling that only comes to visit when I'm with my daughter, or until recently, when Liam Beckett is in the same room. It's a feeling that, even though I shouldn't, I feel guilty for allowing myself to enjoy.

Whether it's the wine, the fact that Molly left a few hours ago with Dani's parents, or the man standing in front of me, all I know is if I don't hold on to this feeling for as long as I can right now, I'll regret it for years to come.

"Megs," he says on a sigh, his fingertips digging in and his eyes swirling with a rich hopefulness that turns those golden flecks you can normally see swimming in his brown eyes into a burning fire lighting his gaze.

Hungry eyes.

I don't think. If I had given myself just a second to process my next move, I'm sure I would have backed out of his hold and run as fast as I could to my car. But, I didn't think, so my next move was pure, one-hundred-percent Megan. But not the Megan I've been for the last couple years since my husband died. No, this Megan feels like I've finally dug myself out of those ashes I've been living in since my life burned up around me. The cloak of depression that normally lingers loosely around my shoulders, dropping to my feet with the feel of Liam pressed tight. I know this feeling won't last, but I suddenly want to hold on to every second I can of this experience, until it leaves me.

I reach out and curl my fingers around his forearms. My eyes growing wide when his brow lifts. With a quick push I rock up and close the distance that is left between our mouths. When my lips touch his, that feeling of being alive burns so bright every nerve in my body feels it, each inch of skin boiling and cooling so quickly it's as if I can't make up my mind if I want to be hot or cold. My hairs stand on end, my skin pebbles—going cold before rushing heat fills my veins, and the very thump of my heart seems to skip a beat the second our lips touch.

One thing I know for sure. I want this. I want this and Liam's going to give it to me.

He doesn't pause. His groan vibrating against my chest only lights the feeling that is firing through my skin. My hands move from his forearms and I run my hands up his chest until both hands curl around his neck and I use the hold to pull my body even closer to his.

His hands move from my hips and he curls them around my bottom, pulling me tightly against his body. When I feel the very obvious sign of his attraction, I moan deeply, and shiver when he answers with one of his own.

I can't tell you how long this kiss lasts. When his tongue moves to swipe against my lips, I open without reservation. We continue, our tongues dancing together while each of our moans are swallowed by the other, until I have to pull away to gulp a breath of air before I pass out—however, the way I feel right now, passing out might very well be a possibility.

"This is finally happening," he snarls in a tone that should scare me, but all it does is act as kerosene to our already uncontrollable fire of lust.

"It is," I agree without question.

"Now," he says.

"Okay," I agree on a sigh and sway toward his hard body.

With the encouragement he needs, his hands finally leave my body. He turns me, wraps one thick arm around my shoulder, and turns to walk toward the front of the house.

"We're leaving?" I question lamely.

"Darlin' I didn't stutter. This is happening," he says, pausing when he reaches the side of the house and the shadows that will give us the privacy we need. His body turns, moving me to stand before him once again. "I need to know you're with me, Megan. I've wanted this since the day I met you, but I knew you weren't ready for me. I've been trying to keep my distance, just waiting for those clouds to leave your eyes. If you don't want me to take you back to my house, strip you naked and fuck you until you can't walk for weeks, then say so now, because the second I have you I won't be letting go."

"Oh, boy," I whisper.

"I prefer *oh God,* but I'll make that the first item on my to-do list."

"You'll make what?"

"My to-do list, Megs. The list of things I've wanted *to do* to you for months now. Making you scream *oh God* will be number one, followed by my name, of course."

"Oh, God," I repeat, my mind swilling with the promise his words inflict.

"Yeah, you're getting it."

His mouth crashes down on mine for a hard but quick kiss before pulling back and giving me another one of those knee-melting smirks. "Last chance, Megan," he whispers while his hands are framing my heated face.

Whatever he sees in my eyes is enough, he gives me a light kiss, takes his hands from my face and curls one around my left hand and pulls me toward his truck.

Liam

Fuck.

I thrust in again, feeling her tight walls squeeze my cock, and roll my hips while I take her mouth with my own. Her moan turns into a high-pitched scream that I swallow. I can feel her release wet my balls when I bury myself deep, again rolling my hips. Her small hands grab hold of my ass and I groan when I feel her nails bite into my skin.

"Next time you come against my cock, you scream my name," I demand, looking her in the eyes. Her eyes widen briefly before they roll back when I thrust deep again. I don't give her time to respond before I power my hips back and take her in a bruising speed. "My name, Megs," I rasp. "Don't you come without screaming *my* name."

She whines.

I groan.

She gives me a small whisper of breath against my lips when I lean closer to her, moving my hips faster.

"Do you want it harder, darlin'?" I question.

"Yes," she whimpers.

"Do you want me deeper?" I continue, pausing when the tip

of my cock is about to fall from her body, smiling wickedly when she makes a cry of protest. "Do you want to feel my cock even when you aren't with me? Want me to take everything you have to give me? So greedy. So fucking greedy." Without giving her a chance to answer, I bend forward and crush my lips to hers. She opens immediately and our tongues meet, causing a fire to race down my spine and curl around my balls.

Damn she feels good.

"Tell me, Megs. Give me the words."

"Take me, Liam. Give me everything. Make me *feel*. God, please make me feel!"

Her eyes bore into my own. With one gaze she is telling me everything her words don't. This means more to her too, I can see it, and fuck me—my body locks tight when I see the depth of her plea.

"Yeah, darlin'. Everything."

She doesn't know it, but with that one word I silently vow to stop at nothing until I make this woman mine.

With one powerful thrust, roll, and push, I give her every-thing I have—over and over. When she throws her head back, it's my name she's screaming loud enough to cause my ears to ring long after her breath grows slow and her face relaxes with sleep.

I lay there looking at her after my cock softens and falls from her body. I remember the first time I saw her, I knew that she would one day be in this position. Naked in my bed and spent from taking my cock for hours. Over the months since that first meet-ing, the feeling, the craving, to make her mine had only grown. I've tried, tried to reach her, but it was clear she wasn't ready. So I waited and fuck me was it worth the wait. Now, having confirmed what I knew then, I know I won't let her go without a fight.

And it will be a fight. That I'm sure of.

But it's also one that I know I'm ready to take on. I know what I want. I know *who* I want.

I also know in order to have those things, I will be fighting the hardest fight I've ever fought.

Because not only am I fighting for someone that can't see through the shadows to find the rope I'm holding to pull herself off rock bottom, but I'm also fighting the ghosts of her past that I'm not sure will let her go long enough to make that climb.

After rolling away from her warm body, I walk to the bathroom and clean myself off, not wasting any time before I move back to my bed. Quietly I lie back down and pull her into my arms. Even in her sleep she curls into me, her head hitting my shoulder, arm curling around my stomach and her legs tangling with my own. I reach down and hike her thigh over my hips and smile to myself while fighting another erection when her wetness hits my hip.

Sitting there, looking into the darkness I know I've finally found her. I've been searching for *her* for as long as I can remember. That person that would make my heart beat faster.

When you grow up with parents like mine, you know without a shadow of a doubt that a love worth fighting for is a love worth keeping. The fight—that drive—the desire to have the person you love, love you back just as fiercely? That's all it's about. They showed me that when you want something, you don't stop until it's yours.

I think I was about eight when I first realized the relationship my parents shared was something . . . different. I was about sixteen when I realized that different was something I wanted. They had some sort of magical power to their love. Nothing that you would ever be able to describe, but when you saw them together there was no denying it. They would look at each other and it was as if there was some invisible cord that connected them completely. Mom would give Dad a smile and he would laugh softly under his breath, always causing her face to redden. He would walk into the room and her whole body would jolt like it had been struck by lightning. Her skin would pebble with goosebumps and she would always snap her eyes to wherever he was. Of course it took me years to understand what that look meant.

They felt each other.

They knew each other past a feeling that could be physically felt.

They had a love that went past anything explainable.

And just like I knew when I first met Megan, she was the person that I would have that with. I knew when I was younger when my person stepped into my path, there would be nothing that could stop me from making her mine. I wanted what my parents had and now there isn't a damn thing that will stop me from getting that.

Megan isn't going to know what hit her.

With that final thought, my lips tip up and I let my body drift off to sleep, while I hold *my* future in my arms.

Chapter 1

Megan

Two Months Later

"TELL ME ABOUT YOUR HUSBAND," Dani asks softly.

I look over to where she's sitting in my living room, reclined back against the love seat, her legs propped up in the seat next to her, and her baby boy, Owen, sleeping against her chest.

I don't answer right away; instead I watch her hand rubbing his small back. The diamonds in her wedding ring glittering against the sun that shines through the window.

Jack.

She wants to know about Jack.

It shouldn't be this hard to talk about him, but even after almost three years it still feels like yesterday sometimes.

"He was my best friend," I tell her honestly.

"Like Cohen and me?"

"Nothing like you two," I laugh humorlessly. "God, Dani, it feels almost like a betrayal to his memory to even admit that out loud. What you and Cohen have . . . that's a love story for the record books. Jack and me . . . well, we kind of fell into love in the most unconventional ways. No, that's not right. We fell in love with each other all because of Molly."

"What do you mean?" she says, her voice just over a whisper.

I sigh, "We grew up together, Jack and I. It sounds so much more glamorous when I say it that way, like we were kids that would run on perfectly paved sidewalks and in each other's backyards until we were called for dinner. But that couldn't be further from the truth. We lived in the backwoods, wrong side of the tracks, trailer park from hell, in a small town in nowhere Georgia with one blinking caution light and the only store for miles was a mom and pop grocery store that, most of the time, only had expired goods for sale. It was hell on earth, really. But Jack, God Jack, he was always seeing the brighter side of life. He had these huge dreams. He was going to get a scholarship to the best football playing college, play for a few years until he was drafted— early of course, or so he would say. He wanted to play with the big boys, Dani, and he could have. He really could have. He was that good."

Dani doesn't talk, but her silence encourages me to finish.

"I wasn't a wild child. Not by a long shot. I was the silent one that flew under the radar and hid in the shadows. Jack was one of my only friends and by far the closest. Had we not grown up next door to each other, I'm sure we wouldn't have even been friends. I was that much of a wallflower. But Jack, despite where we lived and how we grew up, was destined for greatness. The most popular boy in school, captain of the football team, class president, you name it and that was Jack." I smile and look over at Dani, meeting her sympathetic eyes. "My parents were shit, Dani. Not like yours. Nothing like yours. Home wasn't a safe place for me. I'll spare you the details of that because really, you don't want to know. When I got pregnant with Molly, Jack left all those huge dreams he had and joined the Marines, married me, and gave me the promise of a safe and happy love. He knew that he had nothing to offer me with just a pocket full of dreams and by enlisting, we might not have a future he had imagined for his life, but he did what he felt he had to do to protect me. Having Molly turned a love we had as friends and it grew into one that we had as husband and wife."

"I don't know what to say, Megan. I know a bunch of 'I'm so sorry's' aren't going to make it better, but I'm glad that you were able to get out—make a better life out of a bad start. Did he . . . um, did he regret it? Not following his football dreams?" I can tell she doesn't mean this in a nosy way, but just to better understand what Jack and I had.

"Never. Jack wasn't built in a way to ever regret the path his life took. He believed that everything happens for a reason. Although, I'm not sure he would feel the same way now seeing as he died jumping on that new path he dug for his life."

"You miss him," she states without any doubts in her tone.

She would understand, as a wife of an ex-marine she knows what it feels like to live without someone, even though her husband came home, you still feel that emptiness when they're gone. The physical void, as well as the cold hard fear that they may never make it back.

And Jack . . . he never made it back.

"Every day."

And I do. Not just because the physical loneliness, but losing him—someone that I had had by my side every day since I was in preschool—was one hell of a hit to take mentally too.

She nods, reaches her hand over the table separating the love seat from the couch and takes my hand. She doesn't speak, just gives me a gentle squeeze and looks back at the television. I'm sure neither one of us are even watching the reality show rerun that's playing on the screen. I'm lost in my thoughts and I'm sure she is too.

It's hard to believe just how much my life has changed in the course of six years. I went from being a single teenager without much care to what happened in my future, to married with a newborn in what felt like seconds. Don't get me wrong, I wouldn't change having Molly in my life for a second, but losing Jack has changed me. At first I struggled with the will to live, sinking into a depression so deep that I'm shocked I made it out. Molly helped with that. She was my will to live. But even now, after all of these years, I still have days that I sink right back into that dark place. I'm sure a lot of that has to do with the fact that I've never had to be alone, aside from him. Now it's like I've had to learn how to not only live without him, but to live essentially alone.

For the last three years I've been in some sort of limbo. I've come so far from where I was when he first died. Instead of thinking I would never have good days, now I know the bad days come few and far between. His birthday, our wedding anniversary and the date he died are still, and probably always will be, dark days. Moving forward, one foot in front of the other, in the process of moving on. Even though the thought of 'moving on' is still, to this day, laughable. To move on, I would need something to move toward, and it's really hard to focus on the beauty in life when you're stuck living a haunted one with the memory of someone who has been dead for years. Back in the shadows. All those moments that once brought a smile to my face and gave my heart a reason to beat a little quicker, gone. I was reminded, while Dani and Cohen completed that fairy tale for the record books that is their love, how beautiful life can be and as I watched them dance on their wedding night, I found myself wanting that. Craving for a love that deep that I physically ached for it.

And for one night I let myself forget the weights that have held me down.

For one night I lived in the now. I allowed myself to open up and feel all of those things that I have always been convinced I would never have.

For one night I felt the promise of *more* and it scared the crap out of me with the power of those emotions.

Those are the moments that all feel like lead in my gut now. The ones that make it hard for me to push myself past drowning when I dwell on them too long.

Before Jack died we had created a beautiful life. It was a life that held so much promise.

I was, after we were married and left our old lives behind, a phoenix being reborn from the ashes we had left from all the burning pain of our old lives.

All that fire and all that pain, washing away memories we never wanted to have again.

We had been married for two years before he died. It took us a while in that time, to find our way. To feel that promise of a beautiful life. And in that two years I held something beautiful in the palms of my hands. I felt alive.

Reborn.

I didn't live in the shadows around me, meekly praying that no one would notice me.

We were alive and gloriously happy.

I believed with my whole heart that every hardship I ever felt served a purpose because it brought me a happiness that was out of this world perfect.

Until it was gone.

And in its place I was left with a pain that burned so bright I just knew there would be no ashes left for me to be reborn again.

Once again I was stuck in those shadows—that cold place where I was just existing and not living—Molly being the only bright spot in my darkness. It's a painful place to be and it wasn't until Dani and her gang of friends came along that I was able to start clawing myself out of that depression I had sunk into.

So, yeah—it was hard after all that to even think for a second that I would ever feel that promise again. We had come so far and lost so much.

But one night with Liam, I felt it instantly.

That is something I've been struggling with since.

I shiver with the thought and look at Dani, focusing my mind back on our conversation.

"I don't want to be that person I was when we first met, Dani."

She looks back up, her hand jolting against mine, and shock etched in her face. We haven't talked about how I used to be. How bad I was when we first met.

"When I first saw you, at Cohen's going away party, even when I knew what happened to you, all I could see was the sadness. It brought it all back, that night I mean? Made you remember Jack?"

I nod, "It was hard sometimes. I wasn't in a good place back then."

She doesn't speak at first, her thoughts clearly something she is struggling to piece together.

"You're still struggling, I know, Megan. I see it. It hurts me as your friend to not know how to make it better for you."

I smile softly, "I have my bad days, but they're coming far less frequently than they used to. Jack was a huge part of my life and even if we didn't have the same kind of love that most couples do, I loved him more than life. Maybe because he was all I had in mine besides Molly. There isn't a single memory from growing up that doesn't have him in it. I think that's what makes it so hard, when I think about life without him in it now, it's painful to know that the new memories will never have him in them."

"Is that why you won't date? Because of that love you both shared?"

I laugh, this time with humor. "No. Jack isn't why I won't date."

She clears her throat, adjusting herself so that she's more comfortable, and looks down at Owen. "I couldn't imagine my life without Cohen in it. It hurts to just think about it. Even having Owen as a reminder of him would be painful, but a pain I would be happy to have if it meant I held just a small part of him."

Her words rip through me, each one searing me deeply and I fight the gasp that almost escapes. She has no idea how painful her words just were. And of course she wouldn't because even if she is the closest person in my life right now, that doesn't mean I've let her all the way in. God if she only knew.

"But," she continues and I focus back on her, "I know Cohen would never want me to be alone. He would want me to find love again, even if just the thought makes me sick, I know deep down he would be right. You, Megan—you have so much love to give."

"And I give it . . . to Molly." My tone comes out harsher than I meant it to and I can tell that Dani felt the sting of my snapped words.

"You deserve happiness, babe." She smiles, but it doesn't even come close to hitting her eyes. My pulse picks up with the look she gives me next and I know where she's going. Where she's been dying to go since her wedding reception. "I thought for a second you could have found that with Lee."

This time the gasp I held back slips out and I slap my hand over my mouth, my eyes going wide. I shake my head and she looks at me with kindness in her eyes.

"I understand best friends more than you can imagine, Megan. I'm the same way with Lee, well, minus the whole falling in love part." She smiles, the kindness still there, but this time there's something else in her beautiful green eyes. Something that I'm not sure I want to hear. "I see the way he looks at you."

I shake my head and she returns my denial with a bigger smile and another nod.

"Oh, I see it. And I see the way that you look at him when you don't think anyone is paying attention. You two have been dancing around it for almost a year now, Megan."

"All you see is two people that happened to have shared one night of drunken sex and that's it," I fume, finally finding my voice.

"Bullshit." She moves, sliding her legs off the cushion and adjusting her sleeping son while turning to look at me. "You're afraid. I didn't get it. Not until you explained all of that just now. I thought you were playing games, but now I get it."

"Get what?" I ask impatiently.

"The fear."

I look at her. My eyes blinking a few times while my breathing comes in quick bursts.

"You lost your husband and honey, I feel you. I hate that you lost that and although I will never understand what you feel physically, I do know what the thought of a life without my husband would feel like. But you didn't die with Jack and I know he would want you to move on. Do you think he would want Molly to be alone too? You lost your husband, but baby, she lost her father."

Her words wash over me like someone had just thrown an ice bucket over my head. Then as they replay in my mind I feel the blow just as hard as if it was physically thrown.

"Please leave."

Her eyes widen and a soft gasp comes out of her full lips.

"Now."

"Megan," she starts.

"No." I shake my head and will the tears back. "I'm going to go get ready to go get my daughter from school. When I come back out here, please be gone."

I get up from the couch and walk on wooden legs to my bedroom, her words slamming around in my head.

I know I'm being unfair to Dani. She doesn't know how hard the slap of those words hit.

You lost your husband, but baby, she lost her father.

You lost your husband, but baby, she lost her father.

She lost her father.

I stop at the mirror in my bathroom and look at my pale skinned face reflecting back at me.

She lost her father.

I take a deep breath.

You lost your husband.

I squeeze my eyes closed and clamp them tight.

She lost her father.

My pulse speeds up and my skin goes from ice cold to burning hot.

You lost your husband.

My fingers dig into the counter at my hips and I feel one lone tear sneak past my tightly closed lids.

She lost her father.

I open my eyes, look back at my face and feel nothing but rage. Picking up the closest item I can, my hairbrush, I rear my arm back and hurl it at the mirror. When the brush strikes the surface, the mirror splinters and I turn just as the pieces shatter from the force of my throw.

I did lose my husband and when he took his dying breath, I lost every single piece of the only person that ever loved me.

But she's wrong. It isn't the fear from losing Jack that keeps me from opening up. It isn't that I don't *want* to fill the loneliness that I have lived with every day since Jack left—until that night in Liam's arms. No, the part that I struggle with and have struggled with every day since, is the feelings that he brought back into my cold life are so much more powerful than what I ever felt before. Even with Jack. The images of Liam—Liam and me, Molly and us—that had filtered through my mind while I slept in his arms, *they* scared me. I loved my husband, but I was never in love with my husband, and the feelings that Liam Beckett created in my gut have been a burning guilt of that fact since I snuck out of his bed before the sun came up.

She lost her father.

God, if she even knew.

Chapter 2

Megan

I HIT SAVE ON THE DOCUMENT I've been working on for the past few hours and turn to smile at my daughter, her eyes still tired since she just woke up.

"Can I go play with Mr. Axel again?"

I smile, reach up and hold her soft cheek in my palm. She smiles bigger, her dark brown eyes sparkle with happiness.

"Please," she whispers loudly.

"Little bird, I think Mr. Axel has other things to do than play with your adorable self."

Her smile grows and I wait to see what her brilliant little five-year-old mind comes up with.

"He told me the other day I was the prettiest princess in the whole world and I could come have tea parties with him all the time!"

Something about the image of Axel Reid telling my daughter she could come over and have a tea party was just so ludicrous that I burst out laughing, causing Molly to join in and laugh as well. That's my daughter, always smiling and always laughing, even if she is clueless to why.

"Molly, Mrs. Izzy watched you the other night for mommy while I got some work done. I don't think it would be nice for me to ask her to watch you when I don't have anything to do for work right now."

"Sure you do," she states in the most adorable voice and points to my computer.

"Sure I do what?"

She smiles brightly, "Have work to do. I saw you working just now."

Well, I can't very well argue with that.

"Molly, I always have work to do, but that's why I have a schedule so that I can have tons of little bird time and still make my deadlines."

"Deadline doesn't sound like a fun word." Her nose scrunches up and she sticks her tongue out.

"Deadline is Mommy's least favorite word in the whole world. I like peas more than I like deadlines."

Molly grabs her tiny stomach and throws her head back to giggle. And giggle loud. Her blonde ringlets jumping up and down with the force of her hilarity.

"But you hate peas, mommy!" she giggles even harder.

"I know, little bird," I smile and tap her nose.

She doesn't say anything else but just continues to look at me with a big smile.

I smile back.

Waiting.

"So . . . Can I go see Mr. Axel?"

And there it was.

"How about this? How about I call Mrs. Izzy and see if maybe she is free for a few hours and I'll work those nasty pea deadlines I hate so much. But, Mr. Axel might be at work, okay baby?"

She nods her head, those beautiful ringlets dancing again, jumps off my lap and runs back to her room. I can hear her moving around and the sounds of her making what I'm sure will be a huge mess, echoing down the hall. With a deep sigh, I pick up the phone and call the Reid house to see if my darling daughter can spend some time with the two people she has adopted as hers.

Growing up without grandparents myself I know what it's like to want that familiar closeness, so it shouldn't be a shock to me that she's grown so close to them. Axel and Izzy Reid have treated Molly like she's their blood grandchild since before Dani's wedding. If it isn't Molly asking to go spend time with them, it's them calling to see if I need some time to work. It's been a blessing I'm happy to have in my life, but it still feels weird to rely on someone else when it comes to Molly.

But I also wasn't lying when I said that deadlines are something that I hate more than peas, and I hate peas a lot. A whole hell of a lot. With my newest novel due to my publisher in just weeks, it's something that has been stressing me out and affecting my writing. A bad combination for an author. Maybe Molly knows what I need more than I do.

For as long as I can remember, I've loved writing. When I was growing up, I used writing as a way to escape. Now, as an adult, it's much the same—but now I also write for pleasure and not just for companionship.

I published my first book when Jack was deployed the first time. I never, not in a million years, expected my first romance novel to be a success, but here I am five years later with multiple bestseller titles. Writing kept me from being pulled under by the grief I felt when Jack died. It kept me warm when the loneliness became too much to handle. It was, in a sense, the therapy that I needed to begin to heal.

My books got a little dark during the first year after losing Jack, but it's the books that I hit publish on during that time that are some of the most raw feelings I ever, to this day, have put into my pages.

It's not hard to write about fear, loneliness, pain and heartbreak when you're living it. It was through those characters that I was able to start rebuilding my life.

I place the phone to my ear and wait for it to connect.

"You've reached the Reid house, where we can put the plea in pleasure in seconds."

My eyes round and I burst out laughing when I hear Nate's answering voice.

"Give me the phone, boy! Sometimes I wonder if you were dropped on your head," I hear Axel gruff in the background.

"Oh come on, I knew it was Megan!"

There's a sound of shuffling through the line before I hear the phone clatter against the floor.

"You crazy old man!" Nate laughs.

The phone clatters again and I laugh listening to the two Reid men acting like children.

"You two take it outside! Overgrown apes. Hello? I'm so sorry," Izzy's sweet voice comes over the line and I laugh again when I hear the men clearly have not taken things outside.

"Hey. It's Megan," I say between giggles.

"Hey honey. How are you? How is that sweet little princess?"

"I'm good. However, Molly has basically insisted I call because she says Mr. Axel promised her he would be willing to play tea party every second of her life."

Izzy laughs, the sound bringing a smile to my lips. I've been so lucky to have formed such a close relationship with Dani's parents. In the last year they've become family to Molly and me.

"Like you even have to ask," Izzy says.

"You know I do. Plus I know she loves you to pieces, but she was very specific that she wants that tea party and she wants it with Mr. Axel. I swear that kid could talk the heavens into rain."

"If I tell Axel that I turned that princess away he would wring my neck. I swear the older he gets the more insane he is. Molly is a sweetheart, Megan. Bring her over, I'm sure you could use the time to write. Hey, why don't you pack her an overnight bag and we can have a sleepover. I'll have Dani bring Owen over. Maybe a little girl's night is just what you need."

I laugh, "I don't need anything, Izzy. I couldn't ask you to keep Molly overnight!"

"Darling girl, you need more things than you can see." She oddly tells me. "Bring her and bring a bag or I'll lock you out, take her shopping for clothes, and not give her back until tomorrow afternoon. See you soon!"

I pull the phone back when I hear her disconnect and stare blindly at my cell. What the hell?

"Mommy!"

I shake my head and turn from my desk to where Molly is standing. All thoughts of Izzy's strange comment gone when I see she has turned herself into a real life Disney princess. She's wearing head to toe dress-up gear consisting of about five different princess costumes.

My girl, never a dull moment.

"Come on, let's go get you packed. Mrs. Izzy said she wants you all night and just won't take no for an answer."

"Yay!" Molly screams and smiles a huge smile up at me.

Looks like I'm going to have a night to myself whether I want one or not.

DING.

I stop mid-step and turn my head to my front door. I've been back from dropping off Molly for about two hours and in that time I had managed to clean the house and catch up on about two weeks of emails.

DING.

I narrow my eyes and walk to the door. As long as we've lived here, we still don't know our neighbors. They're all older and don't want to be bothered to meet the widow and her kid, which is fine, we've gotten used to it. Since Cohen pulled me into his group of friends it isn't odd that one of them pops over. Usually it's Cohen or Chance checking on things around the house, but with Chance gone I know it's not him. Cohen, since getting married, doesn't stop by as often. I know he's busy, but he makes a habit of coming by and making sure we don't need anything.

He's done that every few weeks since we lost Jack. He and Jack were good friends and I know Cohen uses those visits to make sure Jack's family is okay. I wish I had the heart to let him know how much those visits hurt more than help, but it's on those rare bad days that I slip into that depression that never seems to go away all the way, his visits are just what I need.

And now, having grown into an amazing friendship with Dani and her group of girlfriends, my life is almost bursting with people when before there was no one but Molly.

DING.

"I'm coming," I mumble to no one and hurry to pull the door open.

I pull the door open with a smile and quickly frown when Dani pushes her way in, brown bag in hand and dressed for the club.

"What in the hell?"

"Don't give me any lip. You've been avoiding me and I get it, I over stepped, but it's been two weeks. Mom called, said bring Owen over because you need a girl's night but won't ask for a girl's night because—her words—that girl is stronger than she has a right to be—not sure what the hell that means, other than I'm pretty sure my mom is calling you stubborn. Either way, time to get ready for a night out." She ends her rambling and turns to face me in a huff.

"Uh," I stutter.

"Nope. No timid or unsure Megan now. The girls are on the way so it's time to get your ass ready!"

She holds up the brown bag and my brow lifts in question when I hear the glass clink.

"Liquid courage, my friend."

I laugh, because really what can I do. Dani's going to get her way here or she will just bring the party to my house and I'm pretty sure old Ms. Timmons will shit in her diaper if a party hosted by Dani Cage starts next door.

"Where are we going?" I ask, turning my back to walk toward my bedroom, knowing she will follow.

"Don't know. I guess we'll figure it out when we get there. There's a new club downtown that I've been told is a great place. Ember dragged Maddi out there last week and Mads said it was pretty chill."

"Maddi and I have a different interpretation of chill." I remind Dani.

Maddi—or Maddisyn Locke—is another friend that I met through Dani and I swear that girl is always working some hidden angle. If she's in on this little impromptu party then I know something's up.

"Whatever. It'll be fun. Plus, I haven't had a night without Owen in a few weeks. I love my boy, but mommy needs some girlfriend time."

I glance away from her with a roll of my eyes and head to my closet to try and find something appropriate for going out with the girls to some club downtown.

"That one," Dani says absentmindedly after watching me flick some hangers around and then turns to sit on my bed.

I look over at Dani to judge her outfit before I even dare follow her barked order. She's dressed for a night out, but I'm shocked Cohen let her leave the house like that. She's got on a tight black dress that hits right above her knees with a slit in the middle giving her boobs a highlighted 'v.' The dress is long sleeved so really she isn't showing much, but I know Cohen is the type of man that doesn't like his woman's assets showing and with her still nursing their son, there is plenty of boobage to show.

"Where is Cohen tonight? I find it hard to believe he saw you leave the house in that."

"Of course he did. He's in tonight. Something about a game on television or something."

Had I not been flipping through my clothes I might have caught the look she gave me when she finished talking, but because I was too focused on the fact that I have nothing to wear to a club, I missed it. Probably just as well, because if I had caught Dani Cage in her lie about where her husband is, there is no way she would have been able to drag me out of the house.

Chapter 3

Megan

I PULL THE HEM OF MY dress down. Again. And look over at Dani from under my lashes while I take another sip of my drink. A large sip this time.

"Smile," Maddi says loudly in my ear, causing me to jump and rattle the whole table when I bump into it.

Maddi laughs, throws her hands up, and walks around to the other side of the table. She gives Zac a hug before walking to Nate and giving him one as well. Well, what I'm sure started out as a hug but ended up with her jamming her elbow into his stomach when he pinches her butt. She throws a look over her shoulder at her sister before walking back over to me and picking up her drink.

Maddi—like me—is wearing a form fitting dress. Hers is a light purple color that looks amazing on her tan skin. Her long, black hair is up in a high ponytail and her make up is done to perfection. But unlike me, she doesn't have to struggle to keep her dress from riding up her ass. Mainly because even though she has a great ass, she doesn't have the hips that I do. Which is a major reason why I have avoided wearing anything this . . . tight.

The dress that Dani insisted I wear, ended up being one of the ones that she had her best friend Lyn drag over. Something that they claim they just had, but being that I'm the only one of them that has hips for days, I know they're full of shit. Which was confirmed when Lila, Lyn's twin sister, apologized for being late because they took too long at the mall.

The deep blue dress fit me perfectly. I have to admit it's stunning, there's a thin layer of lace that covers the blue material of the dress and takes it from looking like a cheap bar dress to something a little classier. I should be happy because it covers all the important places, but the low neckline makes me boobs stand out. Then there's the whole back of the dress issue . . . or I should say lack of the back. The blue material stops at my butt and the lace continues about two inches and then it's nothing but skin except for a thin line of blue that crosses mid back, holding it together. A thin and tight chain connecting each side that I'm convinced is going to snap. A very stupid thin line that prevented me from wearing a bra, so with the added joy of being free, I've been praying that my nipples just keep the fun under control.

I tug the hem down again and pull the straw from my drink, toss it on the table, and down the rest of my Long Island Ice Tea.

"Ha! Chug it babe!" Nate yells across the table with a smile. "Wanna see who can drink more?" He challenges.

"Uh, no? Why are you here, anyway?"

"Someone isn't so sure. I'm here because I know you want to play with Nate Dog?" He wags his eyebrows and I cough out a laugh.

"Did you seriously just call yourself Nate Dog?" I hear Stella yell from the corner.

"Sure I did." Nate says and puffs out his chest. "Don't you know how much dogs love to play with cats?"

"What the hell are you talking about?" I inquire.

"Cats, babe. You know, pussy. If there's one thing that a dog can chase, it's pussy. Wanna play?"

"You're such a child," Dani groans and slaps him on the back of his head.

Despite the fact that he has the maturity of a teenager some-times, he does look hilarious pouting at his sister. He reaches up, pulls his shoulder length hair from his topknot and fixes the man bun that his sister knocked loose. Looking at him, strong bone structure, handsome features and green eyes just as stunning as his sister's, I have to admit he's without a doubt one good-looking man.

When he catches me studying him, I get a wink and he thrust his hips, earning him another smack from his sister.

"Leave her alone," she yells.

"Whatever, sis." He holds up his hands and looks back at me with a wicked smile. "So, wanna drink meow?"

I laugh and walk around the table and loop my arm through his. "Sure, big boy, let's go get some drinks. Right, meow," I jest.

I push my arm through his offered elbow, and start to walk

toward the bar. I feel like I have to stand on my toes even with my heels to keep our height even as we walk through the crowded dance floor.

An hour later, I'm pretty sure I've lost the ability to stand up straight. Not because I'm drunk, well . . . I might be a little, but watching Nate work the room with what has to be the worst pick-up lines in the world has me laughing so hard that I've almost fallen over more times than I can count.

"And then he said to her, 'You sure are beautiful. Almost as beautiful as my sister, but you know that's illegal.' And you should have seen her face. She looked like she swallowed a fly. Didn't even take a second for her to turn and run."

Everyone laughs when I finish telling them about one of Nate's attempts at picking up one of the chicks he walked into after our third trip to the bar. Well, everyone except Dani.

"You are so disgusting. I swear Mom and Dad picked you up on the side of the road." Dani turns her head and rolls her eyes at me.

"What? Hey, I called you beautiful. Doesn't that give me brownie points?" Nate holds his hands up and actually looks confused by why we find his failed pick-up lines hilarious.

"Dude, you basically told her that your sister is hotter but you can't do her because she. Is. Your. Sister." Zac says, holding his sides as he laughs as hard as I am.

"That wasn't even the best one!" I yell. "He looked at that

one," I pointed across the room to a tall, stunning blonde before looking at Nate and laughing so hard I almost fall off my stool again. Thankfully two strong hands grab my hips before I can move too far off. I look up at Zac and smile my thanks for him catching me before I fell on my ass. "Then he says to her 'Taco Bell isn't the only thing that's open late and I love tacos' and she," I pause to laugh harder when he narrows his eyes at me, "And then, she said 'baby I've been waiting to have someone offer to play with my taco since I had my sex change!'"

After that, there was no way my laughter could have been stopped. Everyone around us starts laughing and Nate just rolls his eyes and takes a pull of his drink.

"Hey, I love this song."

I jump from my seat and run around the table and into the mass of bodies dancing on the dance floor. I turn and see Dani, Maddi and Stella have joined me as we dance and laugh as each song starts to blur into the next.

We had been dancing for a while now, each of us laughing and having a great time. Nate and Zac seem to be on watchdog duty, because each time someone tries to get too close, they step in. I have a good feeling that they both only showed up for girl's night to keep an eye on us. Or at least they had been until Mr. Cowboy started to get too grabby.

I had just turned to straighten my body after spinning around in a few circles and wiped my hair out of my face with a smile that died instantly. The stranger that we had been fending off for the last five or so songs gives me a sinister looking smile before pulling me into his arms. I look around, frantic, before I realize my spin dancing must have separated me from the group. I can just see the top of Nate's head standing a good distance away from me. At six and a half feet, the fact that I can only see the tip top of his head has me swallowing a hard lump of fear. Being this far away, I know he can't hear me if I call out for him.

I watch Nate's head disappear as Mr. Cowboy starts to pull me further away.

"Hey! Let go, jerk!"

Pulling me against him, he drops his head and puts his mouth against my ear. The feeling of his breath making my skin crawl instantly. When his mouth opens and he pulls my earlobe into his mouth I start to struggle against him with renewed vigor. My fear turns to panic when his teeth bite down on my ear, causing me to scream out—only to have the sound be swallowed up by the loud beats of the music around us.

"I've been waiting for you to come to me," he slurs and pulls me against his hips. I want to vomit when I feel his erection poke me in the stomach. Memories long since suppressed, start to float to the surface and I start struggling harder. I can feel his frustration as his grip on my arms tightens. My arms burn with the strength of his hold and I just know I'll have two nasty bruises.

"I could tell you wanted some of Big Daddy," he moans when I stumble as he pulls me toward the back hall and my stumble does nothing but push me closer to his body. "Yeah, baby. I knew you wanted some of this."

"Let me go," I whisper, the panic starting to close in on me. "Please," I squeak out.

He lifts one hand from my bicep and takes my jaw roughly, his thumb digging into my flesh and he jerks my head up. My eyes water and I let out a whimper.

"You want me. I'll show you what all that teasing your dancing has been doing gets you." He grinds his hips one more time and I almost lose the contents of my stomach.

"What the fuck!"

Before I can even process the move, a fist comes out of nowhere and crunches into Mr. Cowboy's nose. The sickening sound of his bones breaking takes that battle I've been fighting against my stomach to a whole new level. Mr. Cowboy goes back but doesn't remove his hold on my arm so I'm jerked like a rag doll.

"You think about taking my toy and I'm not going to be very happy, pretty boy," Mr. Cowboy says through the blood pouring from his nose and into his mouth.

My stomach heaves.

"Get your fucking hands off her," I hear Nate growl and his warm hand gently goes to the arm that isn't being held. In my mind I picture some sick game of tug of war beginning.

"Fuck you," he spits and in a move quicker than I can process he lunges forward and clocks Nate right in the left side of his face, jerking my body again so hard that my head snaps back and I feel a sting against my back as the chain on my dress snaps.

He doesn't even flinch. I can see Nate torn and not wanting to fight while I'm in the middle of them like some convoluted game of monkey in the middle. Well, that is until the jerk that is *still* holding on to me moves to punch Nate and gets me right in the back of my head.

Luckily for me, he had been drinking enough that the power in his punch was dulled down quite a bit, regardless, my vision swam and between the fear and pain—the battle with my stomach was instantly lost. I lurched forward and spewed every ounce of Long Island Ice Tea I had consumed tonight, along with my dinner, all over that stupid cowboy.

Shock held him still and even though he was covered in my vomit, Zac, coming from behind, grabs a hold of him and started pulling him through the room. I lost sight of them when Nate stepped in front of me and gently tipped my head up. He gives me a quick look, his face stone-cold serious. An expression rarely seen on his carefree face. Seeing this version of Nate jumpstarts the reality of just how serious this situation could have become.

"Come on, Megan, let's go get you cleaned up before the cops get here."

"Cops?" I ask, confused.

"Yeah, babe. You're going to have to give them a few minutes. No way is that douchebag going to get away with trying to force his hand with you."

"What?"

"Megan, are you okay? Jesus Nate, give her your shirt or something." Dani rushes around her brother and I feel her messing with my dress. When I look down I almost throw up again. The whole top of my dress is torn and hanging by my hips. "Your back is red. Did he touch your back?"

I shake my head to tell her it was just when the chain snapped but no words come out. I'm too mortified that my dress malfunction had me exposed during my struggle.

"I saw him pull against the top of her dress. When the back ripped I think it snapped against her," Nate snaps, his tone hard. He's holding on to his anger by a thread.

"What?" she questions.

They stop talking and I feel fabric being pulled over my head.

"Megan, he was taking you to the exit."

I blanch at Nate's words and his eyes widen as I bend forward and lose the rest of my stomach across his shoes.

Between Nate, Zac and Dani, they have me cleaned up and sitting on the couch in the owner's office. Dani hasn't let go of my hand since she sat down next to me. Zac has been off and on the phone since we got in here, standing over in the far corner I can't hear his words, but given that he keeps looking at Dani I think it's safe to bet there will be a very unhappy husband on his way.

I look around the room and try to take my mind off the officer's voice as he questions Nate. It's a nice, clean office, but my skin is still crawling thinking about what could have happened if that man had gotten me out the back door.

I feel dirty.

Not to mention my head is pounding.

"Are you sure she doesn't need EMS to take a look at her?" The officer asks Nate for the tenth time.

I shake my head and hold even tighter to Dani's hand. Nate looks over and gives me a small smile.

"She says no and I'm not about to give her more stress than she needs by forcing it. We'll make sure she's okay."

I glance up and smile weakly at Nate. He gives me a small nod before looking back at the officer. They continue to talk for a few minutes and I zone out. It's been a long time since I felt that helpless rush of fear like I did earlier. The memories that his touch had brought forth are still sticking to my skin. As I think about his hands against my arms, my breathing starts to come rapidly and I feel Dani squeeze my hand.

"It's okay, Megs. It's okay."

I'm not sure who she is reassuring, me or her but I can't form words to respond.

"Where the fuck is my wife?"

I look up at Dani when I hear Cohen's voice thick with rage coming from the hallway. She gives me a small smile and waves at Nate to sit down. I watch as she climbs off the couch and walks over to the office door. When she throws it open Cohen comes rushing through and doesn't stop as his body plows right into Dani. She wraps her arms around him and holds tight as he picks her right off the floor and keeps walking into the room. His head dips into her neck and I can hear him mumbling to her. I tear my eyes away from the intimacy of their connection and turn my head back to the door.

Or I would have looked at the door had there not been a pair of thick thighs covered in dark pants blocking my view. I follow the path of the perfectly pressed material, over the belt—carefully skimming over the gun held at the owner of those thighs and hips—up the trail of buttons on his uniform shirt, until I get to the lightly tan skin on his neck. When I continue my journey I'm met with the dark brown, angry and deeply concerned eyes of Liam

Beckett.

He turns his head—his eyes never leaving mine—and says something to Nate. I hear them talk, but I understand not one word out of their mouths. Shock holding me stupid at the sight of Liam. Until the other officer we had been dealing with sticks his ass into their conversation. I lose Liam's eyes when his head snaps over to where the officer is standing.

"Excuse me?"

"Real lucky we got him, Lee. This guy has got a hell of a lot of people looking for him. Nasty guy. Usually he uses drugs to get his women, but he grabbed her right off the floor. Pretty sure he would have—"

Liam's growl shuts him up, "I would stop talking now, McKnight. Remember where you are when you start speaking freely." He looks back down at me, his dark eyes going from every inch of my face before he takes me in sitting there wearing Nate's huge shirt. "Are you hurt?"

I go to speak, but again no words come out.

"Where the fuck is that bitch? She fucking wanted it. Was all over my dick." I hear coming from the hallway and look up right in time to see the jerk from earlier push off two cops standing inside the office and lunge forward, toward me.

Liam moves, stepping in front of me. Mr. Cowboy doesn't make it far, but his words come flying back and that panic from earlier rushes back to the surface.

"Shit, Megan!"

I hear Dani, but my fear is all-consuming and before I can beat it back, my vision starts to blacken and I sway on the couch.

Chapter 4

Liam

"SHIT, MEGAN!"

I whip my head around and watch as all the color drains from her face. I bark at my partner, Daniels, and don't even wait to make sure they have the douchebag secured. I dip, push one arm under Megan's legs and one behind her back, pulling her into my arms and turning to walk toward the door in the back corner of the office. We've been called to this club enough that we're familiar with the layout of the place. Nate jumps and follows my lead, opening the door to the large bathroom.

"Shut the door," I tell him and wait to hear the click of the door.

"Okay, it's shut," Nate says.

I turn toward him and give him a look that would cause most

men to piss themselves. Nate just holds his hands up.

"Well, fucking excuse me. It's been a long night. You could have said shut the door *behind* you. And maybe said please," he adds as an afterthought.

"Get. The fuck. Out." I snarl in a deadly serious voice.

Once again, Nate tosses his hands up, the white shirt he had under the one Megan's wearing, stretching against his broad shoulders.

I don't turn my gaze from the door until long after Nate had pulled it closed, this time with him on the other side of it. I can feel my breathing coming rapidly and despite the fact that I know I need to calm down before I take care of Megan, I can't seem to ease the fear that I have had since I got the call from Zac. When her small hand reaches up and presses lightly against my chest, I take a deep breath, and let the calm of her touch seep through my skin. Even through my vest, I can feel her touch like a branding burn to my skin.

Turning I look deep into her eyes, careful to keep my anxiety from being seen. She looks up at me, her brown eyes assessing and roaming over my face. I can tell she's trying to place my emotions and it's not something I want to add to her plate. She doesn't need my shit to add to what she must be feeling after almost being taken by a known rapist.

"You okay, Megs?"

"It's Megan," she mumbles.

I close my eyes and drop my head until my forehead is resting against hers. "You're okay," I breathe out in a rush, my body relaxing instantly.

Her body jerks in my arms, but I don't move. When I open my eyes and meet her gaze, her gasp tells me that I'm doing a shit job at hiding my feelings right now.

"Not a call I like getting, darlin'. Scared me to my core."

She pushes at my chest with my words and I wait a beat before dropping her slowly to her feet. I don't move my body away from hers; instead I wrap my arms around her and pull her as close as I can get her with my belt in the way. She struggles, not against my hold, but with where to put her arms. Finally settling with just letting them hang at her sides. I hate that she won't take some strength from me. Dipping my head, I press my mouth against her neck, smiling when I feel her shudder. I don't speak, but when I take a deep breath, pushing the air out in a rush, she shivers again in my hold.

"You've been avoiding me, Megs. I don't like it."

"It's Megan."

I laugh softly, "Yeah, baby."

I don't speak again, just continue to hold her while she shifts awkwardly. Finally with no other option, her arms come up from hanging limply at her sides and wrap loosely around me. My belt digs into her abdomen and I curse the fucking thing for keeping us apart. We don't speak and it takes a few seconds before she pushes against my hold, giving her the space she needs to drop her arms back down to her sides.

I take another deep breath and allow her to fully pull away. Her arms instantly shoot up and wrap around herself in a protective stance that makes my relief from just seconds before vanish instantly.

"This ends now," I state.

"What does?"

"The games, baby. No more avoiding me."

I bend, pressing my lips against hers, but don't move to deepen the kiss. When I back away, I move my hand and lightly caress the marks that asshole left against her pale skin. They aren't going to bruise, but they're fresh enough that I can still see the impression of his fucking thumb and just that mark alone has me wanting to charge through the club to put a bullet through his skull.

"He touched you."

"I'm okay, Liam."

Dipping my head, I move until my eyes are level with hers.

"Not yet, but you will be," I tell her.

I give her another kiss, this time I linger, letting her feel what I wish I could say without spooking her further. When I pull back, I study her eyes before turning and walking to the door. I give her another glance over my shoulder, her eyes wide and her body soft, no longer holding herself in a protective move. With a wink, I turn the knob and walk through the door.

Chapter 5

Megan

"MOLLY, BABY?" I CALL DOWN the hall toward her room, sighing when I don't get a response. "Molly?"

"Yeah!" she screams, running around the corner and crashing into me with a giggle. I wince when her arms reach up and touch the soreness on my arms. Luckily she misses it and with a bounce jumps back to smile up at me.

"What have you been doing in there, baby?" I ask and run my hand through her soft blonde curls.

"Playing," she says with a smile.

"Playing what?"

"G.I Joes. Mr. Reid told me all the tough guys are Joes. He said so. He wouldn't play with my Barbie's, only with the Joes."

I laugh at the thought of big bad Axel Reid playing with anything close to dolls. "Did he, now?"

"Yup! I gotta go!" She turns and runs back to her room before I can even form another word, let alone ask her if she wants pizza for dinner. It's our Sunday night ritual to have a pizza and a movie date, but after her sleepover with the Reid's, I'm sure she's going to be ready to crash early.

After the night I had last night—the one I still feel with every move I make—I'm just too tired to think about cooking. Dani and Cohen dropped me off in the wee hours this morning after we finished up at the club. I waved off their concern and they left worried, but I needed to be alone. The first thing I did was take the hottest shower that I could stand. Then after a few pain pills, I crashed and the only thoughts that had filtered through my mind were ones of Liam.

I walk back to the kitchen and allow a smile to form when I think about this morning when I went to pick up Molly, despite her whines to stay with Mr. Reid.

I wasn't the only one that thought it was hilarious that my five-year-old daughter had wrapped him around her small finger. Izzy couldn't stop laughing. She answered the door with a small giggle and told me to follow her. When I found Molly running a brush through Axel's hair, I joined Izzy in her laughter. Apparently, my daughter had been giving him a make-over for a good hour before I got there. When he turned, red lips and pink blush were all over his face, and he gave me a wink.

"If you think that's funny, wait until you see Nate," Izzy laughed in a hushed whisper.

"Where's Owen?" I question, looking past my smiling daughter.

"Oh, Dani and Cohen were back before the sun was even up to pick him up. I'm shocked they lasted as long as they did," Izzy says with a smile.

"I didn't even have the door all the way open before Cohen was pushing his way in and snatching my boy back," Axel adds on a grumble from the floor.

"This way," Molly sings before putting each of her tiny hands on both of Axel's cheeks and turning his head back toward her. "Do this," she demands and smacks her lips together. "It's not big enough," she mumbles and I laugh when she picks up the lipstick tube.

"Baby, I'm not so sure Mr. Reid will think that is his color."

My face reddens when I think about the burden she's been on them. Molly has always been a child that loves easily and loves big, but usually she's shy around men. She had just turned two when Jack passed away and it's always been just the occasional babysitter until Dani's parents started keeping her. Of course, she knows and loves Cohen and Chance, but even that took her months to warm up to them. It shouldn't be a shock that she instantly connected to Dani's father, the older she gets the more curious she has become, and she has recently been asking more and more about Jack. My heart squeezes when I think about all the things she's missed out on.

"Of course it is, right Molly-wolly?" Axel booms. His voice literally vibrates through the room.

"Get ready for it," Izzy strangely says and I turn to look at her only to have my confusion intensify when she just smirks.

"Where, oh where, is the Princess of Pretty? Oh, Princess! I'm in the need of your magic for I have lost my way! There's no time to waste! The ball is in minutes, no seconds!"

My jaw drops. Eyes widen. And I have to work to keep the hilarity of this moment from bubbling out.

If I thought Axel boomed earlier I was wrong. Because skipping—*skipping on his toes*—comes Dani's older brother, Nate Reid, his voice vibrating through their large living room. All six-foot-something of his muscular frame with a sheet wrapped around his hips as a makeshift dress, and tank top flipped up and folded between his huge pecs to make some sort of weird bra. His make-up is even heavier than his father's, his green eyes even brighter with the amount of shadow my daughter has painted, in what I can only guess is her best impression of raccoon eyes. His lips look like he was stung by hundreds of bees, the red circle of lipstick going from mid chin to the bottom of his nose. But it's his hair that makes me lose the fight to keep the laughter in. He has what has to be twenty ponytails pulling his shoulder length hair up in a million different directions.

He skips toward me, stops and my laughter gets to a level of insanity when he gives me a crooked grin and curtsies before spinning on his feet and falling dramatically onto the floor next to Molly—who is smiling a crooked grin of her own at him.

"Princess, please stop trying to make that ugly troll pretty and tell me where I go to get to the ball! I have to meet the prince before midnight!" Nate takes one thick hand and throws it over his forehead in a dramatic fashion that would give the best actors a run for their money.

"Troll!" Axel yells and kicks out his foot to jab his son in the hip. "I'll show you a troll!"

I watch in fascination as the two very manly men wrestle on the floor, not for one second caring that they're both dressed for a day of drag.

I'm shaken from my thoughts of the morning madness when the doorbell rings. My brow furrows and I switch gears from the kitchen to go answer the door. The only people that would be coming over would be Dani, Cohen, Chance or maybe Nate—after last night he's called a few times to make sure I'm okay. Given that I just got off the phone with Dani, I'm sure it isn't her. Chance would call first and since I know he's going through some personal stuff after the issues Dani had before Owen was born, I know it isn't him. Chance only comes over when he needs someone to talk to, and lately he hasn't been happy when I push for him to go see someone over the depression he's fallen into.

I pull the door open and stop dead.

Liam.

"Miss me, Megs?"

My jaw drops when he shoulders his way into my house and I turn to snap at him when I catch a whiff of pizza.

"What—"

My words die when he leans down and gives me a hasty kiss.

"Pizza."

That's all he says. He holds up the *five* boxes of pizza in his hands and turns to walk through the house. He knows where the kitchen is; he came with Dani, Cohen and the rest of the crew when Molly had her fifth birthday party a few months ago. He didn't say much, but I felt his eyes on me every second that he was there.

"You can't be here," I snap.

He looks over from where he's putting the pizzas down on the counter and rolls his eyes. "Baby, I've been inside you."

He did not just say that.

"You did not just say that, Liam Beckett." My face heats, but not with embarrassment, oh no, he's got me about as angry as I've ever been.

"It's the truth," he says raising one dark brow in a manner that makes me think he's just daring me to give him a fight.

"My daughter is here, Liam."

"You don't call me Lee like everyone else, why?" He questions, while ignoring me.

"You can't be here," I say again, my voice wavering with panic. Molly has never seen me with a man. Well, she has, but never one on one like this. Alone in her home. Mainly because I've never been on a date much less slept with someone since Jack died. She isn't ready for this.

"I told you last night no more games. Knew you wouldn't make it easy for me, baby, but this right here," he stopped to point between him and me, "this is me not letting go. I'll give you last night, even though I don't like it, I was on shift and you needed some time, space. You didn't need me breathing down your neck making sure you were okay. Nate did the calling, kept me in the loop. Cost me, staying away from you when every inch of my body was screaming to come and make sure you were okay. Gave you the day and now I'm here. With pizza," he adds as almost an afterthought.

"With pizza," I parrot.

He nods his head and my anger grows.

"*With pizza!*" I shriek.

"Pizza!" I hear screamed from the other side of my small ranch house and close my eyes in prayer.

Please, *please.*

Maybe she'll forget she heard that and not come in here.

Maybe . . .

Not.

"Pizza! Yay!" Molly comes bounding in the room and skids to a halt when she sees Liam standing with one hip against the island. "Hi," she says with a huge smile.

Liam smiles his knee-melting smile and pushes off the counter. I hold my breath when he walks the few steps over to Molly and drops to her level and holds out his hand. "Hi," he says softly, his smile getting even bigger and even more knee-melting when Molly places her small hand in his.

"You came Lee," she sighs. Even my daughter is easily charmed by that smile.

Wait. What? He came?

"Yeah, little lady, I did. Told you I would," he strangely responds.

She giggles, much to my shock, and pumps her small arm up and down to shake his hand.

"Yup! I'm five. See," she yells in her youthful glee and pulls her hand from his and holds it inches from his face to show him all of her pink tipped fingers. "Want me to give you a make-up-ver?"

She asks with a big smile.

Liam looks up at me with a smile and a question in his eyes.

"Baby, Liam doesn't want you to give him a make-over. He's got to go." I give him a hard glare and hope he gets a hint.

"Go where?" Molly asks.

"Yeah, babe, where?" Liam adds with a smile. That damn knee-melting smile.

"Home."

"Nope. I don't have to go home."

I narrow my eyes at him.

"See! He said he doesn't got to go, Mommy! Wanna do a tea party now?" Molly jumps and spins around the room.

"A word, Liam?" I say through a clenched jaw as I watch Molly turn and grab the doll she dropped when she saw Liam. Making sure she isn't paying attention to us before I return my focus to the man standing in front of me.

"No."

"No?" I gasp.

"Megs, let me be clear here. The only word you want to have is the one that has me leaving and we both know that isn't what you really want. Listen to me and hear it this time. I'm not leaving. I'm not letting you have weeks and weeks of avoiding me. I'm not giving up. And I'm not stopping until you admit to yourself that you see what we could have between us."

"What . . . what we could have?" I whisper and shake my head.

"You need some time to come to terms with it, that's okay, I'll give you that, but you're going to have it with me doing everything I can to remind you what this is."

"What this is? We had one night."

He looks at me. His eyes burn brighter and his smirk turning devilish. "Yeah, I'll give you that one too. But we've also been doing the foreplay dance long before that one night that solidified everything I needed to know, baby. What did that *one night* show you?"

I open my mouth and snap it shut. What am I supposed to say to that? Logically I can argue that we don't know each other, well past the biblical sense, but I know him. Just because I've done everything I can to avoid him because of what he made me feel during the night I lost myself in his bed.

Over and over.

"You have to go," I breathe, my words coming out a hushed whisper that if it wasn't for his eyes going soft, I would have sworn he couldn't hear me.

"Yeah, that's the last thing I need to do. Come on, Megs, come pick out some pizza and let's eat."

With that, he turns, smiles down at Molly and proceeds to charm my daughter with pizza and that damn knee-melting smile.

Chapter 6

Megan

"WILL LEE BE HERE WHEN I wake up, Mommy?" Her lyrical voice is tired with sleep but I can't miss the hopefulness in her eyes.

"No, baby," I sigh.

It's been Lee this and Lee that for the last three hours. One of which I spent throwing daggers at him across the table while him and Molly chatted about everything and anything and the other two while we watched *Frozen,* while he held her in his arms and watched every second. I, however, spent the entire movie freaking out while I watched my daughter become enamored with him.

"But—"

"Goodnight, my princess. Tomorrow I'll make blueberry pancakes, okay?"

She smiles, all thoughts of Liam forgotten with the mention

of her favorite breakfast.

"Love you, Mommy."

"Love you back, baby, to the moon and beyond."

I give her another kiss and turn to leave the room, shutting off the light and closing the door. I rest my head against her closed door for a few seconds before I turn to walk down the hall. Stopping short when I see Liam leaning against the wall at the end of the hall.

"You need to leave," I tell him, ignoring the fact that he watched me and my little silent moment of freaking out.

He doesn't give me a chance to pass him, his hand sweeping out in front of me and curling around my body before pulling me toward him. My traitorous body sings its joy when his skin touches mine.

"We need to talk."

I shake my head and narrow my eyes, which just earns me a laugh.

"Yeah, I can see we need to talk."

"I don't see what we need to talk about, Liam. We had a night, one night, and I'll admit it was good . . . what?" I question when his brow shoots up.

"Good? Baby, that's all you have for me?"

"Well it was."

"Good wasn't when you came against my mouth the first or third time. Good wasn't when your thighs squeezed me so hard I might even have bruises months later. *GOOD* wasn't when you screamed my name, and baby you did, so damn loud my ears felt that for days. Good doesn't even come close."

"Well, it was good."

"No, Megs. It was fucking unbelievable."

His words stop me and I—for the first time—really look at him. His nostrils are flaring and his eyes have turned into that gold flecked burning that brought me to my knees, literally. Good lord, he's serious.

"It's Megan," I say weakly.

"You felt it," he presses, ignoring me.

I shake my head, refusing to give him what he wants.

He tips his head back and I can see his lips moving.

"Are you . . . counting?" I question.

He doesn't answer right away, but his lips continue to move and he is definitely counting.

"Why are you counting?"

His breath comes out and his lips thin. Then to my ever growing frustration, he continues to count.

"Why are you counting?" I ask, again.

He continues before looking back down. His eyes hold mine for a few beats before he looks down at my lips before meeting my eyes again. My breath stalls in my throat with the intensity I see in his eyes.

"I'm counting, *Megan,* because if I don't, I'll take you right here in the fucking hallway. Your baby is right down the hall so that would be a bad idea. I'm counting because I'm trying to have enough patience for the both of us. I'm counting because my damn cock is so hard, I'm not sure how there is any more blood flowing through my body. I'm counting, *Megan,* because I want you more than I've wanted anything in my life and *that* frustrates the shit out of me because you either can't or won't see it. I need you to see it, baby. I really need you to see. I'm counting because since last night, leaving you when I wanted nothing more than to drag you home where I can keep you safe, I've been filled with nothing but worry about how you're handling everything. I guess you could say I'm counting so I don't lose my shit."

I'm shaking my head before he even stops talking and he just sighs deeply.

"Why?" I ask, ignoring the vast majority of what he just said.

I'm not even sure what I'm asking, but clearly he does, because without letting go he turns and leads me to the living room. He stops at the worn leather loveseat letting me go long enough to settle his body before he reaches out with both hands on my hips and drags me down. My knees hit the seat and my bottom presses against his hard thighs. He moves around until he's leaning back and pulls both my hands forward. I watch in fascination as he pulls one of my clammy hands toward his chest. My right hand right above his heart. I try to pull my hand away, but he holds strong.

"Let me tell you something. I've been watching you, Megan. You came into our group kicking and screaming, even if you didn't do it physically, you were resisting all the same. Dani, being all that is Dani, pulled you in and refused to let you go. She has that way about her, always seeing what people need even if they can't see it for themselves. Months. It took months before I saw you even smile. But I still watched. Watched and waited."

"Waited for what?" I ask, the words coming out as shaky as I feel. His heart beating strong and steady under my palm.

"For you to see."

I cock my head to the side and wait for him to continue.

"You saw it that night, baby. And you saw it last night when you went from shivering in fear to a comforting calm just with my hands on your body. I wasn't alone in that bed, Megan, and I damn sure wasn't alone last night."

"It was dark," I say lamely thinking about our night together.

"Yeah and what I'm talking about is something you don't need light to see, baby."

Well, now I'm even more confused.

"You won't get it right away. Hell, you might not even see it, but you will eventually. I've been waiting, Megan and after last night, I'm done waiting. It's time for me to help you *see*."

"See what!" I snap.

"Everything."

That's it. That's all he says. He gives me a smirk, his dimple coming out with his knee-melting smile and his eyes burning bright. I sit there like a dead weight on his lap with my hands still against his chest, his heart beating steady under my palm and try to understand his words.

"Everything? What is that even supposed to mean?"

His smirk grows into a smile. One that has my fingers curling into his skin and my thighs involuntarily pressing against his legs to try and ease the pressure building.

"You'll see."

"Look, Liam. You're a nice guy and all that, but I just don't think you and I are on the same page here."

"Same book, different chapters, baby. Don't worry, you'll

learn to read fast."

"Ugh! I don't think you get it. I mean, I tried to be nice about it. It was sex, Liam. Just sex. I needed it, you gave it, and we both got something out of it. Why can't you just leave it at that?"

He throws his head back and laughs. I literally stop breathing at the sound. That burn in my gut coming back tenfold.

A burn that I haven't felt in so long.

Feelings.

He turns his eyes back to mine and smiles when he sees my expression. "Ah, I see you're starting to understand."

Okay, now I'm getting pissed. I rip my hands from his grasp, instantly missing the warmth of his chest against my palms. I want to kiss him and I want to slap him all in the same breath.

"You don't understand, Liam. I can't . . . I just . . . I can't do this." My nose burns and I can feel the emotion start to climb up my throat, but I beat it down. I try to get up but his hands quickly grab my hips and he pulls me tighter against his lap. "I can't," I choke out, once again fighting the emotions from bubbling out.

"Wrong, Megan. You can, you're just afraid."

"You're fucking right, I'm afraid." My eyes widen when I realize what I've given away. I shake my head and struggle against his hold. His face softens and his eyes don't leave mine when he lifts his hands from my hips. I scramble off his lap so quick that I lose my balance and crash to the floor. He moves quickly to help me, I hold my hand up and give him the back of my head. "No. Don't."

"Megs."

"It's Megan, dammit!" I scream before clamping my lips

tight. "Please, it's Megan. I haven't been Megs in three years, Liam. I need you to get *that* if you don't get anything else."

He doesn't say anything and when I get the courage, I turn and look him in the eyes from my position on the floor. He's pulled his body to the edge of the seat and his arm is still outstretched to help me off the floor. His eyes, they're telling me everything his silence isn't. He gets it and to my shock it looks as if it hurts him just as much as it hurts me.

"I can't be Megs,"

"All right, darlin'. I understand," he says softly. "I need you to be honest with me, sweetheart. Please. I get that this is new, sudden and scary for you. You get me when I say I've been waiting?"

I shake my head.

He sighs, "Can you please let me help you off the floor?"

I shake my head again and use the coffee table to pull myself to my feet, going to sit on the couch opposite from him instead of the chair next to where he's sitting on the loveseat.

His eyes get hard, but as quickly as his frustration was shown, it's gone.

"Yeah, I'll let you have that play, baby. You need to be as far from me as you can to think that will put some distance between us, that's fine. Won't work, but I'll give you that."

"You drive me nuts." I tell him honestly.

"Probably. But I want you to think about it and really think about it and tell me that it's a feeling you don't like."

I narrow my eyes, "Who in their right mind would like being driven nuts?" I ask him, my voice growing higher.

His lip turns up, just the side with that damn dimple, and I harden my gaze. All that earns me is the other side curling up until he is giving me the full force of that smile. Thank God I'm sitting or I would melt in a pile of goo. He smiles at me for a few more seconds before his face grows serious. My chest starts to rise and fall with each breath as he sits there and just looks at me. His dark eyes seemingly see right through me. I curl my arms around my chest and wait. It isn't until he opens his mouth that I lose every ounce of air in my lungs.

"You like it because it makes you feel, Megan."

I gasp.

How? How can he know? How can he have a clue that I, for the first time in three years, felt something other than my love for Molly and I only did that because of him?

"You're getting it. I'm a patient man, Megan. I've waited for you. Waiting for that person that would make *me* feel and, baby, I'm ready. You aren't, but you will be. I just have to make you remember how good feeling is."

"You don't know me," I evade, ignoring his all too accurate nail on the head.

"I know you, Megan. You've been around this group for over a year now. A year of you being in a fog while everyone around you was living. You've forgotten what it's like to live and I'm going to remind you. And while I'm reminding you, all you have to do is feel. Then you'll get it."

"Get what," I say softly.

"Everything."

I open my mouth but close it when he shakes his head.

"It's sudden. You don't get this now, but you will, what feels sudden to you, feels just right to me. I'm not going away, Megan." He pushes off the loveseat and walks over to where I'm sitting in shock, and kneels in front of me. "You were *going to be* mine long before you tripped into my arms at the reception, Megan. You moaned my name as your body greedily sucked my cock dry and I knew you would *be* mine. And you *became* mine last night as I held you trembling in my arms. I've got all the time in the world to make sure that happens. Sleep tight, I'll see you in the morning." He lifts up, gives me a long look until he sees whatever he's looking for and before he's completely standing gives me a kiss on my forehead. "Lock up behind me."

And with that, Liam walks out the front door.

I rush forward when the door closes and turn both the locks before I turn my back to the door and slide down until my ass hits the floor. Looking across the entryway, my eyes take in the pictures that are sitting on a small table across from the door. Right there is a picture of Jack holding a newborn Molly. I look into his handsome face, his bright blue eyes and black hair shaved close to his head, and let the sob that had threatened earlier bubble up.

It's time, Megs.

I close my eyes tight when I hear his voice filter through my mind. Shaking my head back and forth as the tears fall rapidly.

He's right. You need to feel again, Megs.

My eyes clamp tighter.

I miss him. My Jack. My best friend.

It's time, Megs.

The voice repeats.

I pull my legs up and wrap my arms around them.

It feels wrong, after everything that Jack had done for me, to feel this way for Liam. It shouldn't feel like guilt, but it does. I'm still here when Jack is gone. I'm still breathing when he gave his life for me.

He's right. It's time. I need to take this final step and open myself up to live again.

I stayed on the floor until my face was stiff with dried tears. My bottom was asleep and my chest hurt with the force of my sobs. But I finally got up. Instead of going to my bed though, I went to my daughter's room and pulled her into my arms.

My daughter who looks everything like her father even though I wish she looked like Jack.

Chapter 7

Liam

LAST NIGHT I STOOD AT the other side of her door and fought every instinct I have in my body to not break that door down while I listened to her sob. I waited until I heard her tears stop. Then I waited even longer while the lights through her house turned off one by one. It wasn't until I could uncoil my body from its position outside her front door that I was able to leave. Pulling each of the palms that I had resting against the wood of her front door to stand up straight and force my legs to take me to my truck.

Even then it was another ten or so minutes before I was able to turn the key and pull out of her drive. Leaving her tonight, knowing she was in pain, is even harder than it was to walk away from her in the club owner's private bathroom.

I make a mental note before pulling out of her drive that her grass is about a week past the point of really needing to be cut.

When I turn out of her neighborhood I press the button on my steering wheel that will allow me to make a phone call. Wincing slightly when I see it's almost past ten.

"Call Dani home," I say into the silence around me.

"Calling Dani home," I hear before the sound of ringing comes from the speakers.

"Hey," she says softly into the phone.

"That . . . God, Dani," I say in lieu of a greeting.

I don't need to say anything else. Dani has been my best friend since before we were out of diapers. She knows me better than I know myself sometimes. There isn't anything that I wouldn't do for her and the same goes with her.

"That bad?" she asks.

"I knew I would be in for a fight. I knew it, but it still doesn't make it easier to leave when I know she needs me. Do you know how hard it was to wait a full fucking day to come over here?"

"Lee."

"Don't Dani. Don't tell me I might not be the one she needs. I didn't give you that shit when you were fighting for Cohen to see you."

"That's not fair," she gasps.

"How is it not?"

"Cohen and me are completely different and you know it, Lee. Megs is . . . she's been through a lot."

"It's Megan." I say harshly. The look in her face coming back like a physical slap when I saw how much pain that nickname brings her. The nickname her dead husband called her.

"What?" Dani demands, clearly confused with my anger.

"I used to think it was cute how she always corrected me when I called her that. Well, it wasn't cute tonight, Dani. Jack called her that. I have enough against me here, I don't need to be bringing that pain to her every time I call her that. So just don't okay?"

She doesn't say anything for a second. "I didn't know." I can hear her shifting through the line and she tells Cohen she'll be right back before I hear her moving through her house. "She never told me Jack called her Megs, Lee. Hell, I call her that all the time. She's never once corrected me."

"That's because she's locked up tight, Dani. She doesn't tell anyone anything that might cause her to feel a thing."

"She's been through a lot, Lee. Do you think . . . I don't know, maybe this won't end how you are hoping it will."

My fingers curl around the wheel and I let out a deep breath. "That isn't something I can accept, Dani."

"I've never seen you like this Lee. I don't know how to help you when I'm not sure that this is best for you."

"What did you feel when you were without Cohen? When he went overseas that last time? What did you really feel like?" I ask, clearly confusing her yet again with my change of subject because she's silent for a few minutes.

"I felt nothing, Lee. You know that. I felt nothing but pain."

"Yeah? And you knew he was coming back. You were scared for him, understandably, but you knew he would be back. Take that feeling out of the equation and then add three years of locking yourself tight, then tell me what you have left."

She lets out a shaky breath. I hate bringing up when Cohen was gone. I know it was the hardest time Dani ever had. But in order to understand Megan, to understand my fight *for* Megan, she has to go back there.

"I felt nothing, Lee," she sighs, her breath choppy. "I felt like I was living half a life with him gone. Half a life that I knew wouldn't get better without him."

"Yeah, and thank fuck it didn't happen, but if he hadn't come back to you? Then what would you have felt?"

"Nothing, Lee." She stops and I know this is costing her. "I wouldn't have felt alive."

"Bingo, Dani. Bingo."

"She feels, Lee. She has Molly."

"She feels, but she's forgotten what it feels like to be alive."

Dani gasps and I hear Cohen ask her if she's okay in the background. "I'm fine, baby, I'll be just another second, okay?"

"Yeah, Dani-girl. You tell Lee if you're still crying in five minutes I'm going to come kick his ass though."

"Noted, Dani." I tell her and she laughs softly and I hear her give Cohen a kiss.

"What can I do?" she asks after a beat.

"Help me show her that she's alive."

"I'm not sure that's something that can be shown so easily, Lee."

"That's where you're wrong," I tell her and feel that flicker of hope start to burn a little brighter when my plan starts to take form. "Tomorrow, meet me at the house for lunch? I've got something I need to take care of in the morning, then . . . then we plan."

She laughs and agrees, not before telling me I'm crazy. When we get off the phone I take a deep breath and let the surge of excitement that this plan gives me, to douse that flicker of hope until it's a full on burning inferno.

Luckily I have the day off. Last night I had been coming off a two-day run of ten-hour shifts, giving me the next two days free. When I pull up to my house at eleven thirty, Dani's SUV was sitting in the drive. My sweaty skin sticks to the leather seat when I pull my body out of my truck. I reach in and grab my sweat-drenched shirt that I had tossed on the floor earlier and make my way up the walkway to the front door.

"Dani?" I yell into the house.

"Back here in the kitchen. I think something's dead in here."

I smile at her words and make my way toward her voice.

"Yeah, might be last week's Chinese. Or maybe that was two weeks ago."

I turn the corner into my kitchen and see her with half her body in the fridge and two full garbage bags at her feet.

"Christ, how long have you been here?"

"You're lucky I'm not your mom. She would kick your ass for letting things get this gross."

She pulls herself out of the fridge and turns toward me right when I'm about to give her a hug. "Don't you dare come near me when you're wet with sweat, Liam Beckett!" She backs up when I smile and go to do just that. "Hell no, you nasty pig!" She laughs and jumps over the trash bag she had been working on filling up and holds her hands up. "Do it and I tell Cohen you touched my boob!"

That stops me in my tracks.

"First, uh no. Second, not funny. The last time you pulled that shit I had a black eye for two weeks. And I'll add that I didn't even touch your tit, my shoulder brushed against it when we were stuck playing drunk twister."

"Whatever," she smiles.

"Yeah, whatever my ass. You didn't get the black eye AND you spent an hour after it laughing your ass off."

I reach past her and grab a bottle of water out of the fridge. Turning to look at her again.

"Why is there only water in here?"

"You should be thankful I considered that was safe enough to stay. I figured with them being in sealed bottles they could stick around. I thought about calling the CDC in to make sure there wasn't something dangerous living in that fridge!" She throws the towel she had been wiping the fridge out with and I just barely move out of the way.

"So, I've been busy."

"You work too much," she says, changing the subject and grabbing a water of her own before heading to the sink to wash her hands.

"So you've told me, *Mom.*" I sigh.

She sticks her tongue out at me, same old Dani, when she can't think of an insult back, out comes the tongue.

"I have my mom's lasagna cooking and it should be ready by

the time you hose your nasty smelling ass off. Then you can clue me in to why I left my family to come over here." She smiles and I know she doesn't mean it, but I feel guilty for pulling her away.

"Sorry, Dani. I could have waited a day or two."

"Don't be sorry, Lee. You know I'm joking. Plus, when I left my boys were watching a baseball game. They probably won't even notice that I'm gone."

I tip up the water and down the whole bottle in one go. I should have thought to bring water with me earlier, but I was in a hurry to get everything done.

"Where have you been anyway?" Dani asks before lifting her own water to her lips.

"Megan's. Mowed her yard, weeded the flowerbeds and fixed up a few boards that had started to warp on her fence. Stuff like that."

I turn and walk out of the room leaving a shocked face Dani with water dribbling out of her open mouth.

"Jumping in the shower!" I call over my shoulder and head off to get cleaned up.

Twenty minutes later I walk back in to my now sparkling kitchen to find Dani impatiently tapping her foot with her arms crossed over her chest.

"Tell me all of it. Now." She demands with a smile.

"What do you want to know?" I ask, pretending I have no idea what she wants.

"You can't drop a bomb like that and just walk away, Lee!"

"I told you everything. I went to her house this morning, did some work and came home."

"Uh uh," she nods, her smile growing. "And? Did you see Megan? Talk to her? Anything?!"

"Good Christ, calm down." I shake my head and walk over to the table and sit down. "Where's my mail?" I look up and see Dani hasn't moved and now she looks like she's about to come out of her skin if I don't give her something.

"Junks in the trash, bills are over there," she says with a point over her shoulder, "Now speak."

"Impatient much?"

"Lee!"

"You act like I've never been interested in a woman before, Dani."

"Well, you haven't. Not like this."

I pause and think, God she might be right. I dated through high school and college. I had a few serious girlfriends, but no one that I've had to work for it with. And definitely no one that I could see myself bringing home to meet my parents. Megan on the other hand, I can't wait to bring her and Molly home.

"She's different, Dani." I wait for her to sit down before I continue. "You know how it is, you have it with Cohen. It's not something I can describe, I just know. I felt the same way back when she first started coming around. Every time she walks into a room it's like I can feel her. Fuck, I sound like a sappy Lifetime movie."

She sighs and rests her cheek on her hand. I just shake my head and laugh under my breath.

"It is pretty fucking sappy."

"It's beautiful."

"Remember when we got drunk a few years ago and I went on and on about how one day I would find *her?* Well, I did. I found that person that is worth fighting for. The one that makes me excited to just be around her."

"Damn, Lee. How long have you felt this way?"

"I'm not sure. A few months before Owen was born. But I don't think I really understood what I was feeling until your accident." I stop to make sure she isn't having any issues at the mention of the accident that almost took her and Owen from us. "I remember when she got to the hospital she was exhausted from running around all day with Molly with the added panic of rushing to find a sitter. She was a mess. Emotionally holding on by a thread. She sat in the corner and wouldn't move her eyes from Cohen. The whole time she just looked at him with nothing but fear and worry."

I look over from where I had been looking off in the distance of the back yard when I hear Dani sniff.

"She was so alone, Dani. I couldn't just see it, I felt it. I could *feel* her pain and even then it killed me. After Mom and Dad got there, I moved from them to sit with Megan. She didn't speak, hell I'm not even sure she knew it was me she was holding on to, but I held her hand until they came out to tell us what was going on. When the doctor was talking to Cohen I thought she was going to break my hand, she held on so tight. That woman has so much love in her, she's just afraid to give it."

"God, you're gonna make me cry, Lee."

"Anyway, I felt the attraction to her before then, but sitting there in the hospital with her, I just knew. I've spoken to her a bunch of times before then, but at that moment, when I wanted nothing more than to reach inside her and pull her pain away, I knew there was more to it. I've tried to take it further a few times since then. Made my attraction known. Waited for her to take the bait. I didn't have my chance until your reception."

She opens her mouth and her eyes get huge. "You took advantage of her when she was drunk?" she screams.

"Are you serious?" Of all the reactions, didn't think I would get that one from my closest friend. "Tell me you aren't fucking serious."

"Lee, I was there, she had been drinking."

"Yeah, drinking, she wasn't drunk. I see drunk almost daily at work. I know the difference between enjoying the party with a few drinks with a good buzz and shit faced. She was one hundred percent herself when I was with her."

"With her?"

Jesus, this girl.

"What is it that you think would happen, Dani? I practically fucked her on your parents' back lawn!" I boom, getting frustrated.

"Oh, well that was hard to miss." She rolls her eyes and leans back in her seat. "So, you guys went somewhere and hooked up, got it. Have you not seen her since then?"

"She's been avoiding me."

She laughs and I give her a hard look.

"Well, okay."

"I told her last night I was done with the games."

She slaps my arm. "You did that after everything she went

through?" she asks shocked.

"No. I did that when I could tell she needed a distraction to keep her mind from going into self-preservation mode. I did that because when I got that call, I thought that I was going to go out of my mind with worry. I pulled that shit because I'll be fucking God dammed if I let a day go past that I'm not there to make sure shit like that doesn't happen again."

I take a deep breath and remind myself that my anger shouldn't be directed toward Dani.

"Oh. Well. Okay. Now what?"

"Now I figure out how many hoops I have to jump through before she can see past her fear. I understand, she lost her husband and I'm not looking to take his place, but I'm fighting to win here, Dani. I want her."

She doesn't say anything, but I know Dani. She's working out what she wants to say. I stand from the table and grab another water, waiting her out.

"Okay. I think I get it. I mean, I know all about finding that one person and having to fight for it, but I guess I'm worried. Not just for you getting hurt, because as much as I hate to say it, there is a lot of room for you to get hurt here. But, I'm also worried for her and I'm worried for Molly. What happens if Molly gets attached to you, Lee? She's already lost her father and I know Megan hasn't dated since Jack."

"I know. Fuck, Dani, I know. The last thing I want to do is hurt either one of them."

"Then it's time to plan. Let me call Cohen and let him know I'm going to be awhile." She stands up and walks to her purse. I laugh when she gets on the phone and starts to tell Cohen why his wife isn't going to be home until after dinner. I have a feeling the next time I hit the gym with Cohen he's going to try to kick my ass for this unintentional cock block.

"Dani, you should go home." I tell her when she hangs up with a smirk.

"Nope. Trust me, he got what he wanted out of that."

I laugh and try not think about how Cohen is going to win here.

"So . . . what's the first plan?" she all but screams when she sits back down, rubbing her hands together with a weird grin on her face.

"You're way too excited about this."

"It's not every day your best friend—the all but confirmed bachelor—falls in love."

"Do what?" I question.

"Huh? Where are you confused?"

"The love part."

"Such a guy," she gripes. "What the hell do you think is happening here? Awe, I'm so proud. My big boy is growing up! Wait until your mom hears about this."

That gets my attention real quick. "You will not tell my mom anything about Megan and me until there is a Megan and me, got it?"

"Whatever, Lee. Let's go. Come on. Time to plan."

"I'm not in love, Dani." Fuck. It *is* love.

She gets that stupidly weird grin back on her face and nods her head, "All right, Lee. Not in love, got it. So, let's talk game plan."

Choosing it's better to ignore her than continue fighting her on something she's made her mind up about, I move on, but now that she's mentioned it, I know deep down that the feelings I have for Megan are teetering on the edge of love. One thing is for sure; I wouldn't admit it to Dani first. When I say those words out loud, Megan will be the first one to hear them. Love? It's close, so fucking close.

With a big smile on my face, I spend the next thirty minutes explaining everything I know about Megan, how she's been living half a life, and how she is consumed with fear to let more people in. In the end, I think Dani is more confused than she was when we started.

"Dani, she's afraid to feel. Don't you get it? She lost her husband and you and I both know that's the biggest issue here. She was alone long before Cohen and Chance dragged her into our group and even then she was alone until she let you in. Tell me, has she let any of the other girls in?" I wait until Dani gives me a sad smile. "I didn't think so. She might talk to the girls, but you're the only one that she's let in."

"That doesn't mean much, Lee. She might have let me in, but she still won't really talk to me. Not about anything major. I've tried. I know her and Jack were close, like we are close, they had a friendship long before they got married, but past that she doesn't talk about him. I know she didn't have a good childhood—or hell, life before her and Jack got married. No details though. Nothing past the basics."

Jesus, this is going to be harder than I thought.

"One step at a time. First things first, she has to remember what it feels like to be alive, Dani."

"What? What the hell does that mean?"

I smile and I know Dani can see my determination because she gives me one of her own. "Now I bring her back to life. One day at a time."

"You're crazy."

"Nah, more like determined."

"Well, what's this grand plan entail?"

"What's the best way to feel alive?"

"Lee, I don't think you can just have sex with her every time you see her. Things might get sticky . . . no wait, that's a bad word for it. Gross." She makes a gagging noise and wrinkles her nose up.

"Shut it," I laugh. "Not quite, however when that comes she definitely will remember how alive she is. No, I'm thinking more like doing things that make her heart pound. She needs to *feel* and as much as I can't wait to have her in my bed again, that's going to have to wait. Unfortunately."

"You won't last a week."

"Dani, I'll last a lot longer than a week. I had her one night, I know it's worth the wait."

She just smiles before pulling a piece of paper from her purse and a pen before turning back to me. I watch as she writes in her neat handwriting, *Feeling Alive,* and draws a line under it. "Let's go, big boy. Let's make a list of all the ways you can make Megan feel alive."

I laugh and before I know it, we've filled up the whole damn sheet and Dani stands to leave. I look down at our list and smile.

"You're going to have one hell of a fight on your hands here, Lee," she says and wraps her arms around me in a hug of support.

"Yeah, but it's one worth fighting."

She gives me a squeeze and mumbles, "I'm here if you need me."

"Thanks for today, Dani. Go get home to your boys before Cohen comes kicking my door in."

After walking Dani out, I head over to my cell and pull up an empty text screen. I send what I need and with a smile I head to the living room to catch up on Sports Center before bed.

Chapter 8

Megan

I SAVED THE DOCUMENT I HAD been working on when my phone chimes. Molly crashed early, so I had been working for a little while before bed. It wasn't often that I got to work before the late hours, so I was soaking it up while I could. One plus about being an author, I set my own hours. Of course the flip side of that, with each release, it was a little bittersweet because I didn't have anyone to share those moments with.

My phone chimes again and I'm reminded of the text that came through earlier.

Unknown: Your house. Tomorrow. Noon.

What in the world?

I run through my mind who could possibly be texting me when my phone goes off again.

Unknown: Don't ignore me. I'll find you.

A shiver runs through me.

Me: Who is this?

Unknown: Lee, baby.

I drop my phone and listen as it clatters against my desk. Liam. My God, he doesn't give up. I pick up my phone and without much thought, program him into my phone.

Me: I'm busy.

Liam: Don't lie, darlin', we both know you aren't busy. Molly will be in school so don't use her as an excuse either. It's my last off day and WE have plans. Night, doll.

Me: I won't be here.

Liam: Then I'll find you.

Me: Liam . . .

Liam: Megan . . .

I ignore him. If I continue with this bazaar game he seems to be playing then I'll just encourage him. I turn my attention back to my computer when my phone chimes again. I spend a few seconds telling myself not to look. Just ignore it. My willpower lasts all of five of those seconds and when a reminder chime goes off, I snatch the phone up and I can't help the smile that slowly tugs my lips up.

Liam: Sweet dreams, darlin'.

I don't respond. I don't acknowledge the warm feeling that covers me like a blanket either. But I also don't stop smiling until long after those sweet dreams he told me to have had taken over.

Each and every one of them included Liam Beckett.

"Mommy! I want to wear the white ones," Molly whines and points to her dress shoes.

"Baby, not today. Let's wear those when you get home from school. The last time you wore them you had blisters. Remember how bad you said your feet hurt?"

She wrinkles her little button nose and her smile drops.

"How about when you get home we can put on a fashion show? We can both wear our pretty shoes."

Just as quickly her mood changes and a big smile takes over her adorable face.

"Kay!" she screams and leaps up to wrap her arms around my neck, causing me to lose my balance from where I had been hunched down to pull her shoes out of the hall closet.

We both land and laugh before I climb up and finish getting her ready for school. By the time we leave the house we're already running ten minutes behind. I try not to pay too much attention to how beautiful my yard looks now that Liam spent yesterday morning giving it some much needed attention. I definitely don't look at the fence on the side of the house that now doesn't look like it is about to fall apart. I most definitely don't look at my now weedless flowerbed and its addition of a wide variety of new flowers he planted yesterday in a rainbow of colors. Nope. I don't notice any of that. And I for sure don't have a huge grin on my face as I drive away from my now perfect yard.

After I drop Molly off at school, I head to the grocery store to get a good shop in while I don't have an energetic five year old with me. The last time she was with me at the store, she very loudly told me and everyone around the freezer section how her 'gina'—what she calls her vagina—got cold when I opened the door to get some ice cream. That's my Molly. No filter at all.

By the time I finish up my shop it's only nine so I rush home and unload before heading back out to run some errands. Errands I really don't need to run.

My plan is to stay as busy as possible. I have to pick up Molly at two thirty, so I have a lot of time to kill. So I do what every woman does when you need to kill a few hours, just walk into a Target. You could probably lose a decade of your life in one shopping trip, not to mention spend enough money to need a second mortgage. That store, it's my crack.

The last time I looked at my watch, while browsing through their book section and peeking for my own—and finding it—it was almost eleven. Two hours so far spent shopping for stuff I don't need, but now don't know how we got along without them. I mean everyone needs wine sippy cups, right? Well, probably not, but they were cute. I just need one more hour and I can start my ride home. Surely Liam will know I'm serious when he shows up and I'm not there.

I turned the corner to take me to the movies and stop dead. Leaning against the new release section with that damn knee-melting smile lighting up his face, is Liam.

I don't move. My full to bursting cart acting as my lifeline and guard against him. He shoves off and starts toward me, but I back up and move the cart toward him to stop his progress. His smile grows.

"Hey, darlin'."

My mouth waters as his deep voice hits my ears. Not to mention I can feel my sex clenching in want.

"You see, I'm not a stupid man, Megan. I didn't think you would continue to play games though, but that's okay—I've always loved to play. Especially when I can take my time and make sure every single move counts."

Surely he didn't mean that as dirty as it sounded? Right? Something tells me that he knows exactly what his words made me think though, because that smile of his hits a level that is just downright sinful. My knees don't just melt, my whole body does.

"Do you want to play games, darlin'?" he asks, sidestepping the cart and pulling my hands from the handle. "I think you would love the kind of games I have in mind." He whispers and leans down. His hands come up and his warm palms frame my face, his fingertips pushing into my hair and he tilts my head up so I'm looking at him. "I would love to show you some of my games, baby. I guarantee you'll be screaming my name again before the day's over." My mouth drops open and I gape at him as he gives me a wink. His eyes never leave mine as he lowers his head and gives me a bruising kiss.

I don't say a word when he pulls away, all sense of thinking has dried up with that kiss.

"Come on, let's get you checked out. Game time, baby."

Games? Oh. Shit.

Of course, Liam doesn't allow me to pay. Which causes a good five minute standoff in the checkout lane that ends, with him snatching my card right out of my hand with a wink before swiping his own.

He grabs my hand and pushes the overflowing cart with his other, and drags me to the parking lot.

"I'm parked over there, Liam." I snap, pointing in the direction of my car.

"I know where you're parked. As soon as we get to your house I'll have Nate meet me there to get your keys. Don't worry, darlin', when we get done, your car will be safe in your driveway."

"What?" I fume.

"You heard me, Megan. Help me out here without throwing too much of that sexy attitude and let's get these bags in the cab."

The shock of his actions only adds to the fury his determination has sparked in me. I can't remember the last time I wanted to choke someone at the same time wanting them to take me against their truck. I don't think I've ever felt this much raw energy.

"You make me so angry." I tell him and he oddly smiles at my words.

"Good."

"Good? You want to make me angry?"

He turns and looks at me. My feet braced apart like I'm gearing up for a fight and my hands fisted at my hips. I'm sure my face is the mirror image of a raging bull.

"Darlin', angry is the last thing I want you to be. But, as far as I can see I'm doing something right because you, babe, are feeling something."

"Huh?"

"You'll get it soon and once those light bulbs click on I hope to fuck you'll let me show you how beautiful being alive can feel."

He leans over and gives me a kiss against my cheek and with a smack to my rear, he turns and continues to throw my bags in his truck.

With no other choice, I climb into the passenger seat and ignore him while he finishes up. He takes the quickest route back to my house and as I'm slamming the door he laughs before speaking again.

"Darlin' go put on something old. Something you don't care to get a little dirty."

I look over at him and roll my eyes before stomping up the path to my front door. Before I open the door, I notice the perfectly pruned rose bush and my anger dissolves a few notches. Not completely, but hey he did spend four hours working on my yard yesterday, he can't be all that bad.

Tossing my purse on the kitchen counter, I spin and have every intention in ignoring his request, but as he walks in the door, dropping the bags softly on the kitchen table, he turns and gives me a wink.

"Come on, Megan. Unless you want me to get you undressed myself. Something tells me we wouldn't make it out the door if that happens and I would hate to lose our appointment time."

I sigh, "I have things to do, Liam."

"Like what?"

"Work." That should work. You can't argue with someone that needs to work.

"Babe that can wait."

"No it can't." I argue.

He steps forward.

I back up.

His smile grows.

My frown deepens.

"What do you need to work on that can't wait a few hours?"

"Stuff."

He throws his head back and booms out a laugh. I notice my mistake the second his eyes look behind me into the formal dining room. I woke up this morning before Molly to get some paperbacks signed from online orders. I had them all lined up with their invoices neatly tucked into each book. There were, if I remember correctly, twenty-seven individual books lined up on the dining room table, eight more piles of series book orders and that doesn't even count the piles that I had yet to personalize and tag with their shipping information.

All my books. The secret life that I've been able to keep from everyone since Jack had passed away. The part of me that I didn't share with anyone anymore—exposed.

I close my eyes and wait for the questions. I wait and wait, my eyes clamping tighter with each passing second. When he doesn't speak I lift my eyes and look where he was standing, only to come up blank. My heart speeds up and a cold like fear seeps through my veins.

Oh, God.

With a deep breath, I turn, and watch in horror as he lifts one of the unsigned books out of a box I had sitting on the floor in the corner. His eyes take in the cover, a simple dark shaded cover with a heart broken in two with ashes falling from the center. *Bleeding Love* imprinted in a beautiful font that doesn't quite match the darkness of the cover.

And my pen name, Megan Sands, like a freaking neon sign right there on the front.

He still doesn't speak, running his fingers over the cover before turning the book and reading the back. I know what he's reading. I wrote that book when I was at my darkest point. It was the one and only book that I wrote the year that Jack died. In a way, it was the only thing, besides Molly, that kept my head above the water. It was through that book that I was able to find some sort of healing peace with the loss of my husband.

I let my love for Jack bleed out between the loss and redeeming love that the main character, Mia, found when she was faced with a tragic loss of her own husband. I let my mind drift over the plot of *Bleeding Love* and it isn't until I think of the name of the hero that my gaze snaps up to Liam's. How could I have forgotten? Someone up there must be having a field day with my life today.

Mia found her peace with her white knight . . . Liam.

God, shoot me dead now.

Liam, still holding the book, opens his mouth to speak but closes it before his words are formed. I wait, knowing they have to be coming.

I watch in shock as he gently places the book back in the box, letting his fingers linger over where my name is printed, before he walks over to me. His eyes are swirling with questions but he doesn't voice a single one. He takes my face—his fingers lingering over where I had been held by that douchebag last night—between his hands and bends to place a light kiss against my lips. When he pulls back, his eyes haven't lost a single ounce of intensity.

"Liam," I whisper.

"Yeah, baby. We're going to get there."

I frown and he leans forward to kiss the crease between my brows.

"A love worth having, is worth fighting for."

I gasp when I recognize the quote from the back of *Bleeding Love* and I feel my eyes grow wet.

"Go get changed, darlin'," he whispers.

As raw as I feel right now, I don't even fight him. I turn, walk down the hall to my room, and grab an old pair of jeans to pull on with one of my paint tank tops.

Liam doesn't say anything when I return to where he's standing. He takes a look at my outfit before giving me a small nod. "Nate's waiting outside for your keys, grab them for me, babe."

I mutely dig in my bag and hand over my keys. Liam doesn't say anything just turns and walks out the front door. I stand there and look around the room and take in all of my books lining the small area. There is no way he doesn't know they're my books. How can he not have questions?

"Here, throw this on." He tosses a Hope Town Police Department hoodie at me and waits for me to listen.

"Isn't it a little warm for this?" I ask, looking down at the big HTPD block letters across the front.

"You can thank me later," he oddly responds.

"Uh, right." I jam my head into the hoodie and feel my pulse race when his scent floods my senses.

After I'm dressed, he waits for me to set the alarm and lock up, leading me back to his truck, opening my door before making his way to the driver's side.

"Can I get a clue?" I ask meekly.

"Just go with it. Promise me though; if for one second you aren't having fun, tell me. And darlin'," he pauses waiting for me to give him my full attention. "Just feel," he oddly says.

I don't respond. I keep quiet until we pull into the local paint ball center. He parks in the lot and kills the engine. I take in the building, surrounded by a tall fence and look back to Liam.

"Step one, even when you feel pain you can be having the time of your life. You don't have to let that pain be the only thing you feel. The fun in paintball is all in the game. Take that pain and remember, it's only temporary and when you get to the end, the only thing that's left is some colors on your skin that help you learn how to play the game better."

"What game?"

"The game of life, darlin'."

"You make no sense."

"Like I said, it will make sense soon darlin', and I can't wait for you to get it."

He drops out of the truck and walks around to my door. I wait for him and we walk into the center, his hand never leaving mine for a second.

After the longest hour of my life while the owner runs us through the rules and safety procedures, I'm being suited up with more protective gear than the swat team probably wears. I'm not sure how I'm expected to move around like this.

Liam looks over after he adjusts the strap on his own helmet, and gives me a grin. "How do you feel?" he asks me.

"Hot. And stiff."

He laughs and hands over my paint ball gun. I look at it and then back up to him. His grin grows and he walks over to show me how it works.

"I think you got it, darlin', just point and shoot. Just don't shoot anyone on our team."

"How do I know they're on our team?" I ask lamely.

He taps my yellow helmet and then points to his own. "Avoid the yellow."

"Right, avoid the yellow," I gulp.

I kept chanting that as we make our way out the door into the back of the center. The whole thing looks like some weird obstacle course. There are different areas clearly meant to shield and some that look like my worst physical education nightmare come to life.

"Ready?" the owner asks when we make it to the group of ten or so other people all geared up in yellow and blue helmets.

Avoid the yellow. Avoid the yellow.

"When you hear the buzzer, go."

Shit, I missed everything else he said. Liam looks over and gives me a wink through his goggles and when I hear the buzzer sound I watch as everyone scatters. Liam grabs my hand and pulls me toward one of the bunker like shielded areas. It takes me a few seconds to get my head in the game, but when I hear Liam laugh, I watch as he pops his head around the side before pulling his gun up to pop off a few shots. I hear a grunt and then a muted curse before Liam turns with an even bigger smile.

My blood is pulsing through my veins so hard that I can hear it roaring in my ears. I can't figure out if I'm feeling pure fear or excitement. My mind is telling me to run, but the look of joy on Liam's face, transforming him from handsome to panty-soaking gorgeous, makes me want to keep it there.

My hands shake as I pull myself up and peer around the side. I see a few yellow helmets, but my gaze zeros in on one lone blue one with her back to me. With a ridiculous amount of jittering, I bring my own gun up and let off a few pops. When I hit her clear in the back with one of my yellow paint balls the adrenaline rushing through my body spikes, and I feel like my body might explode with excitement.

I can't explain the feelings running through my system. When I drop back down to where Liam is waiting and turn to look at him, the smile on my face can't be stopped.

I'm having fun. So much fun that I don't even think. I drop my gun and grab his padded shoulders and give him a huge hug.

When I pull back, his smile matches my own.

"Let's do this!" I exclaim.

He gives me a nod and for the next thirty minutes I *feel,* just like he asked, and for the first time in a long time, while the adrenaline is rushing around and my heart is about to beat out of my chest, I'm looking forward to every second that is to come.

Chapter 9

Megan

"LET ME PUT ICE ON it, please," Liam asks for the tenth time since we pulled up at my house.

I look over at him with a smile, the same smile that hasn't left since my first hit during the paintball game. Not even when one of the last blue players got me right in the back of my thigh and the burning pain caused me to face plant in the middle of the field. Of course, the pain was easily forgotten when I watched Liam stop and turn sharply and pelt the guy with one try before he dropped down to make sure I was okay.

That smile was shining bright when I watched Liam hand his phone over to the owner, grab me by my middle and position me in front of him. It was still shining huge when his phone came up, flash went off, and I know that had I looked when Liam did, I would see one big wonky smile on my face in that picture.

If the look on his face was any indication, he liked seeing that big wonky smile. He liked it a lot.

I still haven't come down from my high. I look up, smiling at him and shake my head.

"It's going to hurt more if we don't put ice on it."

"I feel fine," I tell him and honestly I am. It's sore, but it doesn't hurt. Well, it doesn't hurt that much.

He looks up from where he's been studying my thigh and gives me a long accessing look.

"What?" I ask him.

"Nothing, darlin', nothing at all."

He doesn't take his gaze from mine. I look down at where he's kneeling against the floor and just drink him in. Today has been the most fun that I've had in a long time. All because of Liam.

"You feel it yet?" he asks after a few minutes.

"Huh?"

He opens his mouth to respond but snaps it shut when the front door opens and I hear my precious daughter laughing at the top of her lungs.

"Mommy! I got to ride in a monster truck!"

My eyes widen and I look at Liam in shock. I had called Dani earlier when it became apparent that my kidnapper wasn't going to give up, and asked her if she could get Molly from school. I know Dani doesn't own a monster truck. The thought of my daughter in a monster truck scares the crap out of me.

"Breathe," Liam says softly.

"Right." I take a deep breath and nod my head, looking deep

into his eyes.

Molly rounds the corner that separates the front hall and the living room, her infectious smile causing me to give her one of my own. When Nate comes into the room, my smile slips slightly.

"You aren't Dani," I tell him.

"Nope. I'm prettier. Right, Mols?"

She giggles and gives him a hug. "Yup! Hi, Lee! Mommy, look, Lee's here!" She turns from where Nate is standing and bounces toward Liam. I hold my breath and wait to see what she'll do next. It seems, if her leaping into his lap is any indication, that my girl is getting attached to all of these men in her life.

I ignore the slight pain in my chest when Jack's face crosses my mind and will myself to not think about the things that he's missing in her life.

"Hey, little lady."

I look away when I see the look of reverence in her eyes. Yeah, my girl sure is hooked.

"Where is Dani?" I ask Nate, avoiding the look on Liam's face as he gazes at my precious daughter.

"She's in time out," Nate tells me, ignoring my shocked face and dropping down to hold his arms out. "What? I'm prettier than that troll, Mols! Has my beauty let you down?" He throws his hand over his forehead and drops to the ground in a dramatic faint.

Molly claps her little hands and giggles at Nate's antics. I swear, this girl.

I look over when Liam laughs and scoops Molly up in his arms.

"Be gone you ugly ogre! Princess Molly has no time for the

likes of you!"

My eyes widen and I watch in fascination as the two huge alpha males play with Molly effortlessly. Of course my daughter is eating up every second of this. I sit there, watching and in the middle of her beautiful laughter I feel like the walls are closing in on me. Not in a bad way, necessarily, but it hits me that this is something that I've been keeping from her. By closing myself off and making it so nothing and no one can come close enough to form bonds that can break, I've also kept Molly locked up.

I've kept my innocent daughter from experiencing relationships of others. Sure, I can justify it away that I'm keeping her from the pain if we were to lose someone else, but what is that teaching her?

My God, I'm teaching her fear.

Fear for the unknown and that fear will keep her from having the beautiful life that I so wish she will have.

With wooden legs, I stand. They don't notice, the three of them having too much fun chasing each other around my living room. Their laughter trails after me as I walk down the hall, into my bedroom, and finally my bathroom. This is the safest room for me to hide away and let the guilt of what my own fear has pressed upon my daughter.

I want to move past this. I know deep down that this is the unhealthiest way of living. I should move on. Jack is gone and there isn't anything that can bring him back. Logically I know that, but mentally I don't know if I can handle jumping over that last hurdle.

It really is time to move on.

Right there in my bathroom, I let the last of my grief over losing Jack bleed out. Knowing that I've been so wrong to stay locked tight for this long. But, just because I've accepted that, doesn't mean it doesn't kill me to let those last bits of fear start to leave my body.

I lean against the counter and focus my thoughts. Looking up at where the mirror used to be, I suddenly can't keep it locked up anymore. But instead of tears, a manic hysterical bubble of laughter comes shooting out.

And then another.

Before I know what happened, seconds pass and I slide to my ass in the middle of my bathroom, hands held over my stomach as the cramps my laughter has caused sink in. Tears blur my vision, and a pain so blinding that makes my breath come in rushed gasps, rips through me.

That's where Liam finds me, of course, the poster child of sanity rocking back and forth on her bathroom floor. If he had any doubts of my mental status before now, I'm sure they're all confirmed now.

He doesn't say a word and as the laughter turns to sobs, he shifts around me and lowers his body to the floor. His legs frame around my rocking body and his strong arms wrap around me tightly. His silence continues as he tightens his hold. He doesn't speak, just lets me lose it in his arms. When I finally calm, he moves us both so that I'm sitting across his lap. His arms come back around me, one going around my middle and pulling me in close. His other arm comes up, hand moving to cradle my face and press me against his chest.

Turning my head, I take a deep choppy breath and let his scent fill my senses. That warm intoxicating blend of wooded pines and leather. All Liam. It fills my head and when I let the air back out, I feel a small sliver of control come back over me.

Almost as if his hold alone gave me some of his strength.

"Molly?"

"Nate's got her, baby," he mutters.

"I'm sorry," I exhale.

"Far as I can tell Megan, that was a long time coming."

"Yeah," I confirm.

"Want to tell me what brought that on?"

I don't want to, but after today—him giving me a day of carefree fun—I feel like I owe him something. Maybe, just maybe, if I let him in just a little he will understand why I'm absolutely no good for him.

"I've . . . I . . . God. I thought that if Molly just had me she would be safe."

His arms jerk, but he doesn't speak.

Pushing my head closer to his body, I take that strength, that safety that his body gives me, and continue, "I never wanted her to know what it feels like to miss someone. Know the pain that comes when part of you dies. That's what Jack was, part of me, of us. She was too young to understand or feel that loss. I guess I've been living in a bubble. Keeping her wrapped tight with me so that we would never have to depend on someone else for *our* happiness."

"Darlin' you aren't living."

"We are," I sigh, "We have each other. But yeah, we—no,

I—haven't been."

"And how well is that going, Megan?"

I pull my head up and look at him, *really* look at him. His eyes hold no sympathy, just empathy. He isn't judging me. As I look into his handsome face, all I see is his understanding, but also his searching gaze boring into my own as if he's trying to communicate something without words.

He's letting me lead.

And if the way his heart is racing against my body is any indication, his holding back right now is costing him.

"She needs this," I confess.

"Yeah, baby, she does, but so do you."

I nod my head and his eyes go soft. His hand moves from where it fell when I shifted to look at him and his other comes from between our bodies. His warm hands take my face and his reverent hold and the tender look in his eyes, causes me to close my eyes.

"Look at me, Megan."

I shake my head.

"Darlin'," he says as his breath dances across my lips. "You need to *look at me.*"

"Why?" I murmur.

"So you can *see.*"

His thumb moves, the pad of his finger running along my jaw. He waits, giving me a few breaths. My eyes slowly open and when I look into his face, just inches from my own, his eyes are burning with an emotion I've never seen directed at me.

I've seen it before and the knowledge of what he's trying to communicate with just that searing gaze, makes my heart leap in my chest before beating so violently it feels like it might break right out of my body. This is a look of complete affection. Tenderness that I've seen a million times since Cohen pulled me into his world. It's one that Cohen is often giving Dani. But right now, coming from Liam, it's mixed with the hunger that is simmering just beneath the surface, his simple look has turned into something I've never experienced, but always wanted and made me yearn to see it a million times over.

A look that no matter how much Jack loved me—it was only a love of friendship and never, not once, a look that made me feel like I was the only person he ever saw.

I gasp, my thoughts feeling like nothing short of a betrayal to his memory.

"You feel it."

My eyes widen and I don't move. Not confirming physically, but giving him that regardless with my silence.

"Yeah, baby." His forehead drops against mine and his eyes stay locked with my own. "You've given that angel everything she needs, Megan. She doesn't lack love, but she has so much to give. She doesn't understand loss, but she will. You can't keep that from her no matter how hard you try. It's part of life. All you can do is be there for her when it inevitably happens. And as hard as this is for you, you have to know that she needs to experience all of the ups and all of the downs that life has. She. Needs. To. Live."

He stops, brings one of his hands from where it was resting lightly against my neck and wipes the tear that had rolled from my wide eyes.

"There is no doubt in my mind that you have been doing the best you can. You protected her while you have been protecting yourself, but it's time to step out of that bubble and let yourself *feel.* Live. You both need this, not just her. You've watched her this past year, Megan. When everyone is around, that little girl lights up. So much love to give. She gives it freely and eagerly. Not one person she comes around isn't affected by that smile."

"I've kept her from this, Liam."

"No, baby. You haven't kept anything from her. You've been too busy guarding yourself that you've missed it. She already has it. Do you really think Nate would have fought his own sister off and volunteered to bring her home from school if he didn't want to? He told me he locked Dani in her own house and brought Molly home, just so he could spend some time with her. Half the time when Izzy is watching her, Molly is watching Nate. Did it seem odd to you that she didn't even bat an eye when I was here the other night? Darlin', those times Dani has had her while you were working? You know Dani and I are close?"

I nod and his smile deepens.

"I look real good in Dani's makeup baby."

My jaw drops and the image of Liam—all very male Liam— the subject of one of Molly's makeovers.

"I'm there, often, and I'll be the first to admit that she has me wrapped around her finger as tight as I can get."

He finishes and gives me a second while my mouth flounders.

"She never told me." My voice comes out harsher than I meant and I can tell he doesn't like it.

"You've been scared of your own shadow for a while now, Megan. She might not have told you outright, but she wasn't keeping it from you."

"Molly never told me," I continue.

"She didn't tell you? Or you didn't want to hear it?"

My brow wrinkles and I think about what he's saying. Had I been purposely been ignoring things I don't want to see? All those times that Dani had watched her for a few hours, she had come home on cloud nine. Her chatter had been nonstop and most of the time so rapid that I couldn't keep up. But—my God! What kind of mother am I?

"Tea parties," I say hoarsely. "I always thought that Leelee was . . . well, not you. That night you came with pizza—" My voice trails off as I remember how my daughter so oddly spoke to Liam like she had been waiting for him. Like she had anticipated his arrival at her home.

"It's not hard to love her, Megan. I would never hurt either of you, but you have to know had I refused the innocent love she so freely throws to everyone around her, that it would have left a mark."

"Why didn't *you* tell me?"

I try to shift, but he doesn't allow me to move from his lap.

"I've been trying to."

"You're so confusing. You haven't been trying to do anything but get back in my pants."

His eyes go hard and he moves so that I can't do anything but look right at him. His eyes burning, but this time without giving me any kind of warm feelings.

"Make no doubt that I would love to be back in those pants, Megan. I guarantee you that the next time I'm right back in those fucking pants it's going to be because you want me there. But don't ever accuse me of using your daughter to get there. The only thing confused here is you. You're too busy trying to keep yourself from seeing what's right in front of you. You've got your-self so twisted in knots to keep everyone out, that you can't see a damn thing."

He stops talking and moves to stand, leaving me with no choice but to follow him up. He straightens, helps me finish my climb from the floor, and drops his hand instantly.

"If I didn't know with all that I fucking am that you're worth the trouble, I would leave and never look back."

I step back a foot at his words.

"So fucking stubborn, Megan. So stubborn. What happened out there," he says, pointing in the direction that Molly and Nate can be heard laughing. "What happened is you finally seeing past the goddamn guilt and fear that has been eating you for years. The fear I can understand, baby, I get it. But the guilt, I don't see it. I've tried to wrap my head around it for months now, and I still can't get it. You aren't living and until you get your head out of your ass you're going to continue living this lonely life. What happened out there was you seeing that, even with you trying to keep her from experiencing anything that may one day cause her a second of pain, she's breaking free of those tangled webs and *living*. Take a page from her book Megan and maybe we can final-ly be on the same chapter. I was wrong before, we aren't just on different ones, you're still ten books behind me."

He turns, looks to where my mirror used to be and even without knowing, I'm sure he's smart enough to put the pieces together. Especially since bits of the shattered mirror are still stuck to the wall.

"Open your eyes, Megan. It's time to grab the rope," he so strangely says before turning and walking through the door.

As I watch his wide shoulders walk through my bedroom I let his words sink in. He's right. I know it. He knows it. The only problem is, I'm not sure I know how to clear a path to the road he wants me to travel on.

He's right. I feel guilt. Probably not for the reasons he suspects, but it's guilt nonetheless. I had a man who gave up everything for me. Hopes, dreams, a career, and eventually his life. A man who gave up everything so that I could escape a nightmare I was living. A best friend who turned into a husband of safety and then eventually one of friendly love. I was content with that, and I know Jack was too.

The part I struggle with the most is the feelings Liam brings into my cold, painful life. They are so much more powerful than what I ever felt for the husband that saved me. The battle I feel within is that Liam, with all his annoying determination, is showing me a promise of something that I know deep down, if I were to lose it, would take me to my knees with a pain I know I could never shake free of.

That . . . that is a terrifying feeling.

But one that I know I need to be brave enough to take that step toward and that hand he's been offering me.

Chapter 10

Liam

I GIVE MOLLY A HUG AND ignore the pain her begging me to stay causes. That little girl could shake me to my core with just one little pout.

"Stay until she comes out?" I ask Nate.

"Yup. I've got a date with the prettiest girl in the world." He looks down at Molly and she smiles huge. Her brown eyes crinkle at the corner and her crooked grin shining bright. "Isn't that right, Molly-Wolly?"

She giggles and I hate that it isn't me she's giving that look to. Fuck me, I'm in deep here.

"Next date's mine, little lady," I tell her and she nods her head, her curls bouncing around her face.

I turn and right when I make it to the door I hear her yell my name, her little voice ringing out and echoing against the walls. I turn just in time to catch her small body before it comes crashing into my legs, reaching down I pull her up and her small arms wrap around my neck.

"I'll miss you, Leelee," she whispers.

I hold her tight and when I look up, I see Megan standing in the hallway with her hand pressed against her chest and her eyes wide.

"I'll miss you too, little lady, so much."

My eyes never leave Megan's. Her pained face the last thing I see before I drop Molly softly to her feet, ruffle her curls and turn to leave them behind. Ignoring every instinct I have to charge in there and demand Megan see what I see.

That together, if she would just grab that damn rope I'm struggling to hold on to and climb, that we—us and Molly—would have *everything.*

It isn't until I pull my truck into my parent's driveway that I realize it wasn't just pain in her gaze right before I left her house. If I'm not mistaken . . . there was also hope.

I climb down from the cab and make my way up the walk to the front door, my thoughts running a million miles a minute. If I'm right, if that was hope, then maybe—fucking maybe—I've finally started to break through the wall that's been separating us.

"Whoa, baby boy!"

Pushing my thoughts aside, I look up and smile at my mom. Her dark hair streaked with gray, her brown eyes holding strong laugh lines, but right now looking at me and seeing right through the smile I've plastered on my face.

"Do you need your mom or your dad right now, honey?"

I reach out, pull her into my arms and give her a tight hug. Her arms come up and hold me close.

As my hug pulls her off her feet, she laughs. "My guess is my boy needs me." She guesses correctly.

"A little of both, Mom. Definitely a little of both."

After I place her back down on her heels, she reaches up and pats my cheek. I look down and give her a weak smile.

"Well, come on. Let's not let any flies in the house. Your dad is out back mowing the lawn. Let's me and you have a chat before he comes and hogs all your attention."

I follow her in, going straight to the kitchen and pulling one of the chairs from the table before dropping down.

"Water, coke or beer?" she asks from the open fridge door.

"Vodka?"

"Ah, I figured this chat would be coming sooner or later."

I look at her, questions clear in my eyes because she just smiles. She doesn't speak as she bends to the cabinet that holds the strong liquor. I watch—and wait—as she fixes my drink before rounding the island and joining me at the table.

"It's Megan, right?"

I narrow my eyes and take a healthy pull, enjoying the way the burn feels down my throat.

"Should I ask how you know this?"

"You could, but I won't give away my secrets. One day, when you're in my shoes you'll understand me when I tell you that a mother always knows."

I shake my head and look down into the glass. Not really seeing anything except the way that Megan looked when I walked out of her door.

"I have no idea if I'm doing this right," I tell her honestly.

"Oh, baby," she starts. "There isn't a right or wrong way to do anything when it comes to what the heart wants. Everyone has to learn that the hard way. Your father and I had to, just like everyone else."

I look up at her words and I feel my brows pull in.

"Don't look at me like that." She reaches up and pushes against the skin between my eyes until I relax my gaze. "I talked to Izzy the other night, that's your freebie." She winks, letting me in on her secret to knowing why I'm here before I could tell her. "Dani fills her in often on how Megan is doing. I don't think it's lost on you that Izzy and Axel have a soft spot for Megan and Molly. They call them their M&M's," she smiles.

M&M's, I smile. So fitting.

"Every step of the way, baby boy. What I haven't seen for myself, is when you two are in a room together, I've heard bits and pieces through Izzy—who got them from Dani."

I look back down to my glass. Damn Dani and her big mouth.

"You know your father had his hands full when he met me," she says and I look back up, meeting her sad eyes.

What is this?

"I didn't make it easy, honey. I could kick myself now for all the trouble I was in the beginning. Really made him work for it and all because I was scared. I don't know what's holding her back, but it wouldn't be a stretch to guess. Fear is a powerful thing, but honey she's also got a lot of loss on her shoulders. All I can tell you is that you're one hundred and fifty percent your father's son and I have no doubt in my mind that you feeling this way, means you know what you want. Nothing and I mean nothing, honey, stands in the way of a Beckett man when he's found that."

I laugh, the sound coming out flat.

"Not sure that she wants that Beckett determination barking at her door, Mom."

"Then I have no doubt in my mind that you, being your father's son, will make her change her way of thinking there."

"I'm trying. God, I'm trying."

She smiles, reaches out and pulls my hand from my glass. "Tell me what's going on. Let's talk game plan, honey."

I give her a smile, matching the one on her face, and proceed to tell her everything that's been going on for the last year. Starting with the feelings I had when I first met Megan. When I started spending time with Molly. How I knew she would be mine long before I confirmed that feeling. And finally how I've been trying to bring Megan back to herself. When I finish talking she has tears in her eyes.

"You've always felt deeply, son. I have to say, hearing how you talk about her and her daughter makes me feel nothing but pride."

I open my mouth, but before I can get a word out, I hear the back door open.

"Wildcat, get your man some water. Damn it's hot out there. I haven't been this sweaty since—" My dad's words die on his lips when he turns to see me sitting with my mom. His gaze, never missing a thing, takes in the serious vibes floating around before he—thankfully—can finish his sentence. "What's wrong?"

"The apple doesn't fall far from the tree, Beck baby." She gives my hand a squeeze, drawing my attention from my father, back to her. "You never give up, baby boy. Never. What you're feeling, that's all going to be worth it in the end. If you need me you know I'm here. I love you."

She stands, gives me a kiss on the top of my head and moves to my father. His head tips down but his knowing eyes never leave mine. He gives her a kiss, turning his eyes to hers. I watch just as fascinated as I was when I was a kid and they would have one of their silent moments. They don't speak, words never needed with them. Her hand comes up and caresses his cheek and he turns his head to kiss her palm. Her skin instantly filling with goose bumps and I know, if I could see her face, she would have that soft look and her eyes would be full of love.

He waits for her to fill a glass of water, taking it from her offering hand, before giving her another kiss and walking the few steps that separated the doorway and the kitchen table.

"Call me later, baby," she tells me and I give her a nod.

I watch her walk through the arch that takes her from the kitchen and to the stairs that lead up to the second floor before I turn and look at my father.

"I knew this day would come."

"Did you now?" I ask, pulling my glass up and draining the last of my drink.

"Always knew it would, I just hope I know how to steer you right, son."

"At this point, I'm not sure there's a right or wrong way to go."

He smiles, his brown eyes so similar to my own give nothing away as he settles into his chair, leaning back and taking another sip of his water.

"Mom fill you in?"

"She filled me in enough. What does she mean about the apple not falling far from the tree?"

He laughs, "Liam, God son," he takes a deep breath. "My guess, you've got a fight on your hands?"

I tip my head, rolling his words around and trying to form an answer. Before I can speak, he opens his mouth and continues.

"I always knew, with how badly I had to fight just to get your mom to give us a chance, that it would come easy once we finally got there. She has and always will be worth every fight and every struggle. I knew the second she came into my life that she was it. One look in a smoky, crowded bar, and I was knocked so hard on my ass I'm sure that I still have the bruise to show for it even now two decades and then some years later."

With nothing but an empty glass, I lean back and wait for him to continue.

"When you were playing ball in high school, what did I tell you?"

Clearing my throat, I say, "That anything worth having is worth fighting for."

"Exactly that. I don't listen much when your mother is yammering on the phone with the girls. I sit back and let her do her thing knowing if she needs to clue me in, she will. So, son, tell me about her."

"Tell you about?" I hedge.

"Megan."

"You sure you don't listen in, old man?" I laugh.

He winks and I laugh. Then, just like Mom, I tell my father everything about Megan and Molly. As I speak, his knowing eyes get bright and I watch as, through my story, my father loses himself in his own memories. When I finish speaking, he clears his throat and drains his glass dry.

"It's like history repeating itself, Lee," he oddly adds when I finish speaking. "Not the exact same, but the foundation built on the same rocky ground."

"Riddles don't suit you," I quip.

"I suppose not when you've got more on your mind than you can keep up with." He studies me before speaking again, "One look, you said?" At my nod, his smile grows. "Buckle up, son, it's going to be a bumpy road."

"I've got four wheel drive," I laugh.

"Liam, I'm really not sure I can add anything here that will help you. As far as I can tell from what you've just told me, you're about ten steps ahead of where I was when I was wearing your shoes. Half the battle is already won. You're in and breaking down that wall, you just need to make sure you're ready to catch her when she falls from that prison she's been living in."

"And if she doesn't ever get to that point? Because I've got to say, I have a hard time seeing the end game through all of this right now."

His hand comes out and grips my shoulder, hard. "That is not an option you give yourself, bud. You don't give up and you damn sure don't allow her to give up on you *or* herself. Your plan's a good one. Hell, it's a great one. But I promise you, it's one that is going to have her hurting before she can heal. From what I know about Megan, she's been given a lot of pain in her life. It's up to you to show her that in pain there is always beauty to be found."

"I don't want to give up on her."

"Then don't. Honestly, son, this isn't about you right now. Sure, in a way it is, but until you get her to . . . what did you call that list?"

"Feeling Alive," I tell him.

"Yeah, until you get her to remember how to live past that pain she's been clutching tight to, then you need to hold on and gear up. What's the next step?"

"Number two on the list was karaoke."

His brows furrow. "What in the hell is there about karaoke that put it on the list at number two?"

I smile, feeling that determination that I had started to lose come back.

"You have to learn to laugh when you feel so scared that you just want to run and hide. You have to hike those big girl pants up and even though you want nothing more than to run back to your little bubble of safety, and push through the fear to let yourself dance to the music."

He smiles and I look into my father's eyes and give him a big grin of my own.

"Proud of you, son. She isn't going to know what hit her with my boy working that Beckett magic."

I laugh, "I hope she doesn't. Thanks for the chat, Dad. Love you."

"Love you too, bud. Now tell me how much you hate those ten-hour shifts."

We spend the next hour talking about how my shifts at work are going now that I'm on patrol. He tells me how things are going down where he works at Corps Security and as always reminds me that he wishes I had decided to come and work for him and not joined the force.

By the time my mom joins us we'd moved into the living room, beers in each hand, and the television on the sports channel. I don't leave until long after my mom had filled my stomach with a meal fit for a king and a calming sense of purpose to get my girls.

Chapter 11

Megan

*I*T'S BEEN A WEEK SINCE Liam stood at my front door and hugged my daughter goodbye.

A week of silence from him.

A week of me missing him fiercely.

A week of realizing that continuing to push him away will be fruitless, because in this week I've craved him with an unhealthy degree.

It baffles me that he could be under my skin, so deeply imbedded this soon. While we've known each other for almost two years—or at least that's how long it's been since I was first introduced to everyone at Cohen's going away party. In that two years we've been thrown together at various parties, group nights out, and basically whenever Dani pulled me out of the house when I would get too consumed with work. For the last six months of those two years though he hadn't hidden his attraction. Little touches here and there, the casual brush of his skin when he would walk by, or most recently—after Dani and Cohen's wedding—our shared night of the hottest sex I've ever had.

I think it was during the paintball game that I realized he had started to burrow under my skin. When I looked at him, his knee-melting smile shining bright, and felt my gut get tight . . . that's when I knew how much trouble I was in.

Then he held me in his arms while I completely lost my shit and ever since I felt his arms wrapped tight around me in comfort, I've been craving that feeling for every second of every day since he walked out my door.

"What are you thinking about that has that frown making an appearance?" Dani questions.

"Just thinking," I tell her.

I look up from where I had been signing the last of my book orders and look around my dining room table. She isn't focused on me, instead on packaging the last book that I had slid her way. I watch as she handles the paperback with so much care, her eyes rolling over her fingertips as she touches the glossy cover. Moving my gaze from hers, I look over at Maddi and Stella, who have been helping me get together my weekly mail outs.

This—having them in this part of my life—was a huge step for me this week. It was part one of my plan to let those walls crumble and what better way than finally letting them see *all* of me. Dani, of course, knew but it was news to the other girls.

"Thinking about Lee?" Maddi probes.

I take a deep breath, "Yes."

Dani stops what she's doing and snaps her eyes to me, causing me to laugh.

"Shocked I admitted to it?" I jokingly ask.

"Well, uh . . . yeah."

"She's played stupid long enough, figured one of these times she would open up," Stella mumbles.

"Do you want to talk about it?" Dani continues, ignoring Stella's comment.

"Yes," I breathe.

Her eyes widen a fraction because she carefully closes her shock down. Or maybe it's excitement. Either one, what my friend is not hiding is her happiness that the subject isn't being dropped.

"So, all right. Let's do this," Maddi exclaims, rubbing her hands together.

I laugh, letting some of the nerves leave my body. These are my friends. I'm safe here. They won't judge me and they won't think badly of me. I keep reminding myself that there is nothing to be afraid of as each of them sit back and wait for me to speak.

"Uh," I stammer. "So you know he's been . . . persistent?"

Maddi laughs, "Is that what we're going to call it?

"Okay, maybe adorably annoying with his determination would be better?"

They all laugh at me and my nerves ease instantly.

"Don't keep us waiting, Megan! What is going on up there?" Maddi asks on a laugh, reaching over the table to tap me lightly against my temple.

I swat her hand, enjoying the easy banter between us. Sobering slightly, allowing the serious thoughts I had been having minutes earlier to come back, I look at each of these girls that have come to mean so much to me.

"Things got a little intense last week," I start. Each of them lose a little of their smiles. "I guess. . . . well, I—damn this was so much easier to word in my thoughts."

"Just start from the beginning, babe, can't see a better way to clue us in on what's weighing heavy on your mind."

I give Dani a small nod and a weak smile when she stops talking.

"The beginning, right." I look over at Maddi and Stella. "Do you two know about . . . did you hear that we, uh, had a little sleepover?"

They look at me and I can tell they're both struggling to hold onto their laughter. Did I just really call it a sleepover?

"I hope it wasn't little," Maddi belts out, causing Dani and Stella to erupt in giggles as my face heats to a roaring burn.

"Oh, God!" I clasp my hand over my mouth and shake my head.

"Is that a no? It wasn't little?" Stella giggles.

I look at her and narrow my eyes. "For your information, not that it's any of your business, he is far from little. In fact, he was so, uh, well endowed, he had to really work at it!"

Shit. Dammit. Did I really just admit that?

"Explain," Stella says, leaning forward, her face the picture of seriousness.

"No, please don't," Dani gripes.

"Ignore her. Finish. Explain."

"Jesus, Stell . . . that's Lee you're talking about."

"Lee has a dick, right. He's always been selective with who he dates and you know just as well as I do that he didn't bring anyone into our group so I never got to grill anyone. I'm curious, screw me. I bet he's hung. He's hung, right?"

"Do you want a tissue for that drool?" Maddi mumbles and rolls her eyes.

"Maybe, I don't know yet. Finish!"

"This is so embarrassing," I tell Stella, then look to the other two girls. "If you don't want to hear it, cover your ears or leave the room."

Dani instantly pulls her hands to her ears and starts humming, loudly. Maddi makes not one move to shield her hearing; she just cocks her brow and waits.

Looking back at Stella with burning cheeks, I give her what she wants. "He was so large that he had to work me over twice with his mouth, then again with his fingers. By the time he finally gave me every single thick inch of himself I should have been embarrassed with how wet I was. Happy?"

Stella throws her head back, her recently dyed purple hair falling in a thick wave of curls as she laughs at the top of her voice. Maddi on the other hand is just smiling and nodding her head. When I look over at Dani she looks like she might puke, obviously she wasn't humming loud enough.

Pulling her hands away, she looks at Stella. "You are sick, my friend. God, I'm never going to be able to look at him the same again."

My face flames even brighter.

"There isn't a thing you should be getting so worked up about over there. Jesus, Megan, you would think you were a virgin with all the blushing you're doing."

I narrow my eyes at Stella.

"I told you what you wanted to know, no need to be rude now."

"I'm not," she says in an offended tone. "I swear. I just want you to feel comfortable with us. Promise."

Maddi reaches out, all traces of joking gone from not only her supportive gesture, but also her expression holding nothing but understanding. "He was—please don't think I'm being insensitive here—the first? Since Jack?"

I nod.

"There isn't one thing that you can't talk to us about, you know that?" she continues and waits for my confirmation that I understand before opening her mouth again. "What was Jack like?"

Given the subject of our chat, her meaning can't be missed.

Step two in knocking those walls down, here I come.

Time to stop holding back when it comes to telling people about my past.

"Timid," I tell them truthfully. "The first time we had sex it was so awkward. We had been nothing but friends, but with where we were at that point in our relationship, it was the next logical step."

True enough, I tell myself.

"And after that first time?" Maddi requests, clearly deciding she's the self-appointed leader of questions since I opened up to her first.

"A little less timid, but still awkward." Instantly I feel my stomach start to cramp. Admitting how our relationship had been to myself had been hard enough, but letting others know is a whole new level of painful. Not to mention it feels like I'm stomping on his grave mentioning how unfulfilling our sex life was. "I loved him, but we were probably the most dysfunctional couple in the history of ever inside the bedroom." My words come out quickly. Just like ripping off a BandAid.

I can tell they don't understand. Of course they don't, *they* only know half the story.

"Okay," Maddi coughs. "So, I'm going to go out on a limb and say that those times you were together were few and far between? I mean no disrespect, I promise, I'm just trying to understand."

I give her a small smile.

Give them more, Megs. It's okay.

I shiver when I hear Jack's voice in my mind. Well, not his voice, I'm sure. If my mind wants to play tricks on me so that I keep going, fine. I can't go back to the old Megan.

Baby steps.

"He was deployed during most of my pregnancy and was only home for two weeks after her birth. He shipped back out again and the only other time he was home was for a few months when she was one. He died during that tour shortly after Molly turned eighteen months. Needless to say, he was gone a lot, but even when he was home . . ."

I trail off and remember those times he was home. Those times had been all about Molly. He loved her so ferociously. We did things as a family and when Molly had been asleep for hours, we did what we had always done best, spent long hours just enjoying the other's companionship. Hours spent reading to each other, him enjoying some of my books or whatever project I was working on, sometimes just helping me hash out some plot point I had been stuck on. He was huge on board games. We would spend so many hours just laughing over whichever game we had picked up.

What we didn't do often was have sex.

"We slept together the night before he shipped off . . . that last time, and that was almost four years ago."

Dani reaches up and brushes a tear off her cheek.

"I loved him," I meekly say in Jack's defense. And I did.

"We know you did, babe. No one here thinks differently," Maddi speaks first and the others nod in agreement.

I take a huge breath. Then another. Then I speak again. "That night, with Liam, I felt the earth move."

Stella snorts when Dani gags and just like that, the heavy mood is lifted.

"Go on," Maddi encourages.

"The way he touched me. The way that felt. The way *he* felt. All of him. His strong body covering mine made me feel delicate . . . fragile. And the way he talked to me, my God the way his words alone worked me up should be illegal."

"Okay, so Lee is good in bed, can we *please* move on!?" Dani snaps.

"Figured he would be," Stella laughs and sticks her tongue out when Dani huffs.

"So then what happened?"

I look over at Maddi and smile. "Paintball happened."

She gives me a look, not following. Stella gives a 'huh' and Dani oddly smiles all wonky.

"Did you say, paintball?" Stella questions.

I smile, mine feeling just as wonky as Dani's is.

"Well, I guess the bar night happened first. He showed up and laid it out that he was done with me avoiding him—which I had done since that night—and thus began the annoying persistence."

My smile, which had started out smallish on the wonky scale, was full out cheek hurting now.

"The next day he had told me he would be around my house at noon. I, of course, made it my mission to be gone. He tracked me down at Target an hour before noon and, well . . . then paintball."

Maddi tilts her head. "Paintball?"

"It was the most fun I had had in years, Maddi. It's like Liam knew just what I needed. The rush, that feeling of adrenaline tipping over until you're so full of it that you might explode, it was incredible."

"All right, so paintball," Stella stammers. "So weird."

"Then what happened?" Dani says a little too excited.

My cheek-burning smile slips. Then Dani's follows.

"Then I proceeded to flip out after he brought me home. Well, after Nate had brought Molly home."

Dani's shoulders drop. "I know, I told you I was sorry about that, but you try fighting off a man over a foot taller than you when he locks you in your son's bedroom and yells through the door that he's taking the cutest girl in the world on a date. I swear, he kidnapped her right from my house." She crosses her arms over her chest and leans back in a huff.

She had explained to me earlier in the week that her 'time out' had been more like Nate imposed jail time while he stole my kid. I can't be mad about it. I know Molly is safe with him and he took her carseat out of Dani's car so that she would be safe in his truck.

I give her a smile, "It's okay, really. Molly loves Nate and honestly it was the best thing that could have happened."

"Now explain *that!*" Stella gasps.

With my eyes never leaving Dani's so that she knows I mean what I'm saying, I continue. "Seeing Molly, so innocent and happy while playing around with Liam and Nate, I realized that by keeping myself closed off from everyone, that I was keeping her locked away from those relationships too. I was, in a sense, keeping her in that limbo I was in. Long story short, she brought it all to light while two grown men acted like my house was a wrestling mat. It was time for me to move on. So, yeah . . . I broke down and Liam found me losing my mind on my bathroom floor. He wouldn't give up either. I may have come to the self-realization that I was teaching my daughter to fear life, but he hammered the nail home when he helped me see she was breaking free no matter how hard I held her back. I was just too far in my head to see it."

They don't speak but I can tell the room had lost all traces of earlier hopefulness. It dawns on me, in that moment, that they haven't just wanted me to hook up with Liam, they *really* want me *with* him. They've been rooting for us long before they let on to it.

"It's okay," I tell them. "I'm okay."

"Sorry, babe, but all that doesn't really give me the reassurance that you're okay. We worry about you," Dani states.

"I really am, Dani. It hurt, God it hurt, but it needed to happen. Things got a little heated between us, and not in the good kind of heated. I said some things I didn't mean and he once again was all Liam. Fully honest and didn't hold back. He gave me the words I needed to help me take the final step."

Dani's brows curl in, her beautiful face turning from worried to confused. "Final step to what?"

I hear Liam's parting words filter through my mind and with a smile I tell them, "Grab the rope."

Chapter 12

Megan

AFTER THE HEAVINESS OF OUR conversation earlier, the girls all agree that we need to lighten things up. Mainly, Dani decides that we need to have some time to just relax and laugh.

So that leads us to now. Another attempt at girl's night, this time it's more like girl's night plus chaperones.

We decided to head to a local bar that caters to more of a mature crowd and not so many college kids looking to get drunk.

Mike's, has been one of the places that we've often spent a Friday or Saturday night. The music is always good and the bar is big enough that a group our size has enough room to lounge. The bar opened about four years ago, from what I understand, and since its opening night, has been one of the top karaoke joints north of Atlanta.

I never joined in on the actual singing, but it really was too much fun to watch some of our crew get up there and belt it out like they didn't have a care in the world.

Dani called Lyn and Lila to see if they wanted to come before we left my house to head over to the Reid's to drop Molly off with their parents. Lyn was all in, but Lila had plans already and promised to come next time. When we got to Dani's parents, Cohen was already there and after we said goodbye to the kids, we headed out. When we got to Mike's, Zac, Zac's little brother Jax and his girlfriend, Ivie, had been waiting in the huge back corner. It was blocked off like some kind of VIP area, holding two couches and four chairs that formed a closed off square.

Zac, always ready to have a good time, was surprisingly quiet without his sidekick, Nate. We got a chin lift from Jax, but otherwise he was too busy keeping the blush on Ivie's face. She gave us a wave, but was distracted when Jax shoved his hand up her shirt. They were sickly cute, high school sweethearts that everyone was convinced would be married before they graduated college.

I used to see them and just hurt with how close they were. Same with Dani and Cohen, but now—it's so much easier to see their love and not feel a pang of depression wrap tightly around my neck. The fact that I can see them now and feel nothing but happiness that they've found that person that makes them whole, is a testament for how far I've come in the last year.

I look around our little corner, sip my third heavy-handed drink, and let myself enjoy this newfound sense of life. One where I'm able to laugh a little easier and sit a little straighter without that damn cloak of pain holding me back. I can't explain the way that feeling makes me feel. It's like I'm reaching for something and I'm just a touch away from it. Like my glass is just a breath away from being full. I guess that's part of healing the gap, in a sense. I'm almost there—so close—and I've never felt better.

Well, that's a lie.

I close my eyes when Liam's face pops in my head. His eyes bright with happiness and that smile that makes me weak at the knees blinding me with his power. I let my lips tip up with the thought and slowly let my lids open.

And gasp.

"Boo, darlin'."

I look down at my almost full glass, trying to figure out if I had enough drinks that I'm starting to hallucinate. Surely I'm not drunk enough to be conjuring up Liam's face just a breath away from my own.

The couch dips and I move my eyes from my drink to the large body that joined me. My view is blocked temporarily by a tan arm that is corded with muscle as it comes up slowly. My eyes follow the limb as it moves up and over before I lose it and feel it's warmth like a burn when the weight settles against my shoulders. When I move my gaze down from where the arm had been, I see Liam's handsome face so close to my own.

He doesn't say a word before his handsome face moves and his lips touch mine lightly. "Hi," he breathes against my lips.

"Hey." My voice comes out on a wisp of air. I know with the music floating around us that there's no way he could hear me, but his smile grows all the same and I have to shift in my seat when the throbbing starts between my legs.

"Don't you two look all cozy like? Any room for this stud?"

My eyes don't leave Liam as he turns and flips off Nate. I study his strong jaw, stubbled with hair. My eyes roam over his skin drinking him in with every inch. When he swallows, his jaw clenches and I can feel my body responding to just that small movement. His hair is stylized in that sexy way, the thickness tamed with whatever product he shoves in it, slightly longer at the top and I just know he effortlessly must run his hands through it, almost as an afterthought while getting ready.

His head turns and those dark eyes of his meet mine. He studies my face for a beat before one brow arches, and if I didn't know better I would swear he could hear my thoughts. He knows, with just one small look, how badly I want him.

My hunger spiked so high, I'm mad with my cravings for his body.

When a shiver runs through my body, one corner of his thick lips tip up and he gives me a small nod before turning his head back to the group.

Mutely I turn and stare at Dani across from me on the other couch, where she's settled on Cohen's lap. She gives me a wink and I watch as her hands come up, thumbs sticking high, and relax slightly as a laugh bubbles up from deep in my belly. Liam's hand, the one resting against my shoulder, curls into my skin and my eyes widen, as my panties get wet with my arousal.

It's going to be a long night.

With no choice but to run with it, I give the new Megan a mental shake and vow to take each moment as it comes.

Fifteen minutes later, a new drink in my hand, and I'm faced with the first test to my newfound resolve of living in the moment. The old Megan, the one living in fear, would have bolted the second that Liam was called to the stage. But the new Megan, the one that's determined to climb the rope and leave rock bottom for good—that new version of *me* is shocked still.

Never, in all the times that we've been here, has Liam taken the stage. And I knew before I started coming out with them, that he hadn't done it before me either. Nate said once, after spending an hour trying to convince him to sing *Baby Got Back* with him, that he never goes up there because he is as tone deaf as it gets. I remember the moment like it was yesterday. Liam just nodded and turned his gaze back to the stage. But I also know from being around this group long enough that despite his over confident demeanor, Liam Beckett has a mean phobia when it comes to being in front of a crowd. Something that Dani has had way too much fun with in the past.

That knowledge is what holds me to my seat. When he stood from the couch, I instantly felt his loss and my body moved to the edge of my seat, almost as if it was trying to stay connected when I lost his weight against my side.

When the opening to Van Morrison's, Brown Eyed Girl fills the air, I gasp. Liam, with all the confidence in the world, takes the mic and opens his mouth. His voice ringing out around us, booming through the speakers, hits every note as if the song was written just for him.

Perfect pitch.

His body moves with the beat and even with a song like Brown Eyed Girl, Liam's movements look nothing short of sexual to me.

My heart speeds up and I know, without a doubt, that he's planned this moment just for me.

You're my brown-eyed girl.

As I watch him work the crowd like a pro I feel like I'm about to jump out of my skin. The need to have those hands, the ones that are holding the mic to his lips, on my body is burning me alive.

He keeps singing as he jumps off the small stage and makes his way over to our area. I can see our group eating this up. Clapping and singing along with him as he takes the final steps until he's standing right in front of me.

"Hell yeah," Nate yells and grabs the mic when Liam hands it off before the song finishes and I hear him belt out the end of the song as the crowded bar gets even louder.

"Darlin'," he pants and reaches out a hand for me to take. I don't move. I can't imagine what my face looks like right now, but whatever he sees brings a smile to his lips the likes of which I've never seen before. "Take it, baby. *Take my hand.*"

With a trembling arm, I reach up and finally take his hand.

Chapter 13

Liam

I MIGHT PUKE.

If the churning in my gut is any clue, it might be soon.

Fuck, this better work.

When I hear my name called out, I shove that feeling aside and make my way to the stage, tagging the mic from Todd, the announcer, and waiting for the music to start.

Never once taking my eyes from where Megan is sitting.

Fuck, this better work.

She's moved since I stood, her ass just about to fall off the edge of the couch. Her lips parted slightly and her eyes holding me captive.

Yeah, baby, I'm sure you didn't see that coming.

When the song starts, I instantly forget my hatred for being on display like this and look at Megan as if she is the only woman in this room. She might as well be. As I jump from the stage and make my way to her, making my intentions clear as I keep my eyes locked to hers, I'm rewarded with seeing her eyes light a fire and that desire I've been waiting to see, start an inferno. Her chest is moving rapidly when I take the mic from my mouth and shove it blindly toward Nate.

This is it.

Moment of truth.

I know, from Dani, that Megan has been living a little lighter since I left last week. I also know, from her help conspiring to get Megan here tonight, that it's a green light, full steam ahead for number two on our list.

The rush that's flying through my body from my little moment in the spotlight is making my breath come out in pants, but I keep on, eyes on the prize as I reach out and hold my hand out for her.

"Darlin'."

Her eyes go from my hand to my face. I wait for the panic to wash her features, but when I see a hunger that could rival my own take over, I feel my body relax and with a grin stretches my lips.

Thank Christ.

"Take it, baby. *Take my hand.*"

To anyone watching I'm sure it looks like the simplest of gestures. But I know, I fucking know, if her hand hits mine that she finally sees what I've been waiting for. That she is ready. Ready for me to give her everything.

I hold my breath. The magnitude of what this moment means hitting me like a tsunami.

This. This is it.

When her soft skin comes up and even through her trembling movements I know, my girl is ready.

Time for number three.

"Time to go," I tell her and she nods. It's small, but she nods. I bend down, grab her purse and turn without saying a single good-bye to our friends and walk out the door. Not with Megan behind me, nervous or scared, but with her matching me step for step as we head through the bar and out into the warm Georgia night.

When we reach my truck, I unlock the door and help her into the cab, handing her her purse after she clicks her belt. She looks in my eyes and gives me a smile, not timid at all. Her smile is strong and sure.

"Ready?" I question.

She closes her eyes, clears her throat and her smile grows, "Yeah, Liam. I'm ready."

"That's my girl."

I lean forward, hands pushing into the soft hair around her face and I curl my fingers, giving her the slightest pressure before I press my lips to hers in a kiss that demands her compliance. It's a kiss that shows her without words what's to come.

Breaking the kiss, I press my forehead to hers and pray I can get through the next step without my rock hard cock taking control.

Soon. But not yet.

I round the hood and jump into the driver's seat, turning to look at her as her fingers run along her swollen lips. She moves her head and when her eyes hit mine, those lips tip up and a care-free excitement takes hold of her nerves and I breathe easy know-ing I've finally broken through.

"Where are we going?" she asks as my truck bounces through the dirt path we turned off of just seconds before.

"A little late to ask, darlin'," I joke.

"Well, I don't think I was able to form a sentence that would make sense until just now."

"Yeah?"

"You, Liam, kiss me stupid."

My laugh comes out quick and I turn to look at her for a sec-ond before returning my eyes back toward the dirt road before us. I know this road like the back of my hand, but in the dark I know better than to take my attention away for too long.

"Stupid isn't how I want you."

"How—how do you want me?" Her question is just above a whisper and the quiver attached to each word works my cock so well, she might as well have wrapped her lips around my shaft.

I can see the clearing just ahead and I wait until the truck's parked before I answer. Turning slightly, I reach out and with one finger pop her seatbelt free. Her eyes follow my hand and as the fabric of her seatbelt moves across her chest she pulls her arm free and lets it clang against the side of the truck.

"How do you want me, Liam?" she repeats, her body moving

slightly so that she can see me better.

Reaching out with both hands I grab her hips, curl my fingers into the soft skin and pull her toward me. She helps, just as eager as I am to be closer. Her legs move, straddling my lap, and when the weight of her body settles against my lap, we both moan. My hands, still at her hips, pull her toward me in a rocking motion that has the heat of her pussy warming my erection to the point that I'm questioning if I just came a little.

Her small hands come up and wrap around my neck. "How do you want me?" she says with her lips moving against my own.

My tongue comes out and I trace the curve of her bottom lip. When her mouth opens slightly, causing her lip to move closer to my mouth, I nip it with my teeth, pulling it slightly before letting go. Her eyes hood and her hips rock forward against my hold, causing my fingers to dig in tighter.

"Tell me, Liam. How do you want me?"

Rocking her against me again, I watch as her head rolls back and I bring my head toward her exposed neck. Running my tongue over the soft skin from her collarbone until I reach her jaw, where I once again give her a soft nip.

"Do you feel it, darlin'?" I ask, ignoring her repeated question.

Her head tips forward and she nods.

"No, baby. Do you *feel* it?"

She takes a few stuttered breaths and as I wait, I run my hands from her hips, up the tight material of her black tee and when my hand passes right under her pits, my thumbs roll over her erect nipples before I continue my path, until my hands curl around her neck and I pull her head forward until she has no choice but to look at me and only me.

"I want you, darlin', to feel. That feeling your body gets when it's sparking at every nerve. When your skin feels tight and your stomach drops. When you don't know if your heart is beating in your chest or coming through your throat. I want you to feel that wind in your hair, pulse racing, wild, free as a bird, stomach-dropping rush. I want you to feel," I pause, bringing my lips to hers in a soft, eyes-open, kiss, "*everything.*" I finish and close the distance again.

Her mouth opens instantly and when I push my tongue inside and meet hers, the kiss goes from wild to electric. Her hands slide into my hair and she grabs hold and pulls me as close as I can get while her hips move without reservation. A kiss that is dangerously close to having me rip her clothes from her body and taking what I've been craving.

I pull back when I feel my balls start to pull tight, ripping my mouth from hers as we both pant rapidly.

"Fuck me," I groan, tilting my head back and fight back the orgasm that almost had me coming just from dry humping.

"I want that," she whispers.

"Words, Megan. You want what?"

"Everything."

"Well, thank fuck."

Chapter 14

Megan

"THIS WAY, DARLIN'," LIAM TELLS me as he walks us from his truck and into the darkness. I know we're in the middle of nowhere. As his truck pushed through the dirt path and into the clearing you could just tell there wasn't anyone around for miles. When his headlights shut off and you could see millions of stars light up the sky like little gas filled flashlights, it was confirmed. No way you would see something that beautiful, a sky so clear, there wasn't one single spot you couldn't see for miles, if there was even a town close. I would guess, seeing as we didn't pass a single house for at least five miles, that there isn't much of anything out here.

"Uh, Liam?"

He stops and I almost slam into his back.

Turning, his hand comes up to hold my cheek against his palm and I search through the shadows around his face to find his eyes.

"Trust me?"

"Yes," I tell him instantly.

His fingers spasm against my skin.

"Finally."

That one word warms my belly and I roll onto my toes and touch my lips to his.

"I wasn't ready yet, before I mean."

I don't know where all this newfound strength is coming from. If I had to guess, it's all because of the man standing in front of me.

"Yeah, darlin', I know you weren't. You took my hand. That told me everything I needed to know, but that doesn't mean it isn't good to hear you tell me."

"I'm sorry."

Time for me to take that step. The last one I need to climb from my old life and on to the new path full of hope and promise.

Letting the darkness be my shield, one I know I don't need against Liam, but one I'm going to hold on to as a safety blanket regardless, I take a deep breath and knock some more of that damn wall down.

"The way you make me feel, it scares me. It's a good feeling. A different kind of fear. More of an unknown. Never, not once in my twenty-three years have I ever felt a connection as strong as I do when I'm with you."

He drops the hand he had been holding onto and moves to wrap both of his arms around me. His chin rests against the top of my head and he doesn't speak until my arms circle his waist.

"The last thing I want to do is scare you, Megan. That's the last feeling I want you to have when I'm here. What scares you?"

"That's a long story, Liam."

"Lucky for you I've got all the time in the world when it comes to you."

I tighten my grasp on him and soak up the way his embrace fills me whole.

"Every time you're around me I just know I'm that much closer to falling way too quick. It's something that I know if I let happen, I'll tip over the edge in a free fall that I wouldn't be able to pick myself up from if I lost it."

His arms go tight, his body solid, and I take a second before continuing.

"You, everything that is you and the promise of you, is something I'm terrified to take because you hold the power to crush me. You hold all of the power here."

I feel his head move as he shakes it lightly.

"Yeah, you do. And it isn't just me, Liam. You wouldn't just be crushing me, but Molly too. I let you in and it isn't just me I'm giving you. I'm giving you a little girl who I've known for a while now, but only just come to terms with, is so desperate to give *her* heart to someone to hold."

"Darlin', you give me that and there is no way I would throw the world away when I hold everything I want in my hands."

"You say that now, but—"

He pulls back and I silence immediately.

"I say that now because I have no doubts. Megan, I'm not just some stranger you just met. You know me. I've gotten to know you as much as I can. You opened yourself up to me for one night and I knew with no fucking doubts that I would fight until I was blue in the face for this chance. I've watched as you've come alive, baby. You had me hooked before I even said one word and everything I've discovered about you over the last year and a half just dug that hook deeper. These few weeks, seeing you grow and *heal* took that hook and dug it so deep it hit bone. That was all you. All I did was give you a little push."

He pauses, but I know he isn't done when his finger comes up and silences my words before they can leave my lips.

"You spend one second with Molly and you're in love. Doesn't matter if you're a stranger on the street or a man with his own desperate need to give *his* heart to someone to hold. Wouldn't be a hardship to take what she so willingly gives, darlin'. I want that. I want this. I want you both. Please tell me you can see that."

"I see it," I utter as my vision clouds with tears.

"You see *what*," he implores his tone just a hint away from begging.

"Everything," I choke out.

He doesn't say another word. His body relaxes instantly against mine and before I can blink, I'm pulled flush against him and his mouth is against mine. I gasp, breathing him in as he uses my shock to deepen the kiss further until I'm not sure where I end and he begins.

Our hands roam over each other's bodies in a frantic pace. I slip my hands under his shirt and moan when I feel his warm, soft skin against my fingers. It's an odd mix of silk and steel as I move my hand over the ripped muscles of his back and sides. My fingers dig in and try to find purchase when he bends slightly and with his hands flexing against my bottom, he pulls me up and my legs leave the ground to wrap around his hips.

"I had plans, Megan," he moans against my lips. "Have a list of things I need to check off, but right now that has to wait."

"Wait for what," I breathe, kissing a path from behind his ear and down his neck.

"For me to make you mine."

He starts walking, back the way that we just walked. I continue to let my lips learn his skin as he moves to open his truck. When he drops me lightly into the passenger seat, I whine from the loss of his body. Bending forward, his lips find mine again and when he pulls back, the dome light above our heads illuminates his face.

"Last chance," he tells me with a wicked grin. "And this time I mean last one, darlin'. We take this step and make no doubt about it, you will be mine. You give me this and I fucking promise you that I will never make you regret taking that step. You ready to jump from that chapter you've been skimming through and skip into mine?"

I give him a smile, one that is full of confidence and not the least bit unsure as the words that he had told me weeks before come back between us.

"I'm ready."

"Fuck," he groans. "Buckle up, baby."

My smile doesn't slip for a second. Not when I pull my belt across my chest. Not when he slams the door and races to his own. It grows wider when he slams the truck in drive and fishtails back onto the path that will take us back toward town. It isn't until his big hand reaches out and takes my leg in his strong hold that my smile slips slightly, but it only slips because my head falls back and I whimper and try to rub my legs together to ease the ache between them. I lose the smile completely when my mouth drops open and that whimper turns into a loud whine as his long fingers dance up my legs until he slips beneath the hem on my shorts and pushes my panties to the side, pressing against my clit in sure movements that have me panting in seconds.

"Fucking drenched," he grounds out through his tightly clamped teeth.

I roll my head against the headrest and look across the cab at his face. His finger dips from my swollen clit and as he drops his hand lower, his wrist twists slightly so that when he gets there his finger slides deep inside me.

My legs spread instantly when his thick finger fills me and I hear his rumbled groan fill the space around us as he slides his finger as deep as his position allows before pulling it back, then repeating his movements until I can feel myself soaking his hand. If he keeps this up, I won't last. He adds a second finger and my hand digs into the door and I reach out, wrapping my other around his forearm and choke on shattered breaths when he thrusts his fingers so deep, I feel like I've been electrocuted as he hits *that* spot that has me panting, whimpering and begging incoherently.

"Please, Lee, please," I pant. How I formed those words, I'll never know.

"Fuck," he snarls, the sound making my arousal spike even higher. "You'll call me that when I'm so deep inside you my balls will be soaked with this sweetness."

His fingers curl and I pant, my hand cramping around the force of my grip.

"Please, oh God. Not without you, please."

I pray he understands my plea and when he curses, I know he gets me. His hand leaves my pants and I cry out, causing him to spit out a string of curses that would make a sailor blush. His leg slams down and I feel the truck pick up speed as I watch him take his fingers to his mouth and lick every drop of my wetness from his skin.

"Holy shit," I exhale.

"You're getting my mouth first, darlin'. That wasn't enough of a taste and fuck me, I'm starved."

I say nothing, just continue to feel like my heart is about to slam from my chest as I continue to shift my legs back and forth in attempt to ease the burn he's lit between my legs.

Chapter 15

Megan

LIAM PULLS THE TRUCK UP his short drive and doesn't waste a second turning the key and ripping it out. His door is thrown open and I watch immobile as he stomps around to my door, my head tracking his every movement.

When my eyes meet his through the window, I shiver with the intensity that is written all over his face. My door opens and his hand snakes out, unbuckling my belt and pulling me from my seat with strong gentleness.

Of course, that gentleness is gone the second my feet hit the ground. He hands me his keys and without a word, I'm in his arms and he is prowling toward the door.

"Let us in, darlin'," he grumbles and I falter when his mouth starts to lick and nibble down my neck. When I don't move, he pulls his mouth from my neck and grunts, "Need you to open that door before I fuck you in the yard, Megan."

"Oh, okay," I sputter.

He dips his head again and I feel his body shake with silent laughter. "Only you could make me laugh when I'm so hard it hurts."

"Oh."

"Yeah, oh. Let us in. Now."

His mouth takes control of my neck again and with a shiver down my spine, I reach out with his keys and unlock his door, turning the knob to let us in. The sounds of his alarm beeping hits my ears and he steps through, kicking the door shut behind him before moving us toward where the waiting alarm panel is.

"Two-Nine-Six-Two," he grumbles against my skin.

My hand is shaking so violently, I almost don't hit the right combination. The second his alarm is settled, he turns and takes the stairs two at a time. His hold never falters as he then stomps through his hallway and into the darkness of his bedroom. Walking right up to the edge of his huge bed, he places me against the mattress, and shifts his body as his hands come out to grab my hips and spin my body until my legs are dangling off the edge.

I watch as he lifts his arm, grabs a fistful of his shirt and pulls it over his head. Each inch of his golden skin making my mouth water as the moonlight through his open window hits his muscular torso. I reach out, running my hand down his abs and lick my lips.

"You can play later," he tells me as his hands then move to push mine out of the way and toward his buckle.

The second he releases the leather and his deft fingers start to pull each button from their secure hold, I have to fight the itch I have to rip the material from his body. I can see his thick shaft pushing against the denim as he works to free himself.

His hands leave their mission and I watch as he stands, thumbs hooking his briefs and jeans before he gives me a crooked grin and bends to push them both down, before straightening once again. Then he gives me a blink to take him—all of him—in before kneeling on the floor in front of me. I look down my body at him and he licks his lips.

"Now. Now you get my mouth."

Oh, God. The rush of arousal overpowering my already over-loaded system.

His hands reach out and I jump when he palms the skin right above my knees, earning me a smirk. He takes his time, killing me with the slowness that his hands take as they travel up my thighs. Right when he reaches the top, his thumbs brush against the crotch of my shorts and I almost come unglued, my hips jolt-ing off the bed. He moves quickly then, moving his hands to my hips and pressing me back down before curling his fingers into my skin.

"The smell of you, God damn. I thought I was starving for you before. I'm going to eat you until you can't breathe, Megan. Fucking drown in you."

"Oh, God."

"Hold on, darlin'," he tells me and then my shorts and pant-ies are flying over his shoulder, his hands back at my hips and he pulls me against his mouth—hard.

My head falls back and I lose the strength to hold my body

up. When my back falls to the mattress, his hold gets tighter until I'm being pulled to the very edge, with my ass hanging half off. One of his strong hands leaving my hips and curls under my leg to throw it over his shoulder, fitting his mouth even tighter to my core.

When his tongue starts to twist and push against my clit, I cry out and he grabs my other leg to pull it over his other shoulder. Then in a move that would make a porn star proud, his mouth opens wide and his cheeks pull in as he sucks hard while his tongue drops down and pushes inside of me.

That's all it takes for the burn to catch fire and sear through my body in an explosion that puts stars in my vision, and my breath to stall in my throat. My back arches and my fingers ache as I fist his sheets between them.

He hums his approval against me just when my climax starts to ebb and I jump right into a second spike of pleasure, screaming until my throat burns. His head twists and his stubble burns against the sensitive skin on my thighs. My hand moves from its hold on the sheets and I push my fingers through his thick hair and try to move his mouth from its delicious torture against my swollen skin.

He growls against me and shakes his head, making me whimper when I feel the movement shoot up my spine.

"Please," I gasp.

He doesn't move, only intensifies his movements.

True to his words, he doesn't let up until I've come another time against his talented mouth and only when he's licked every inch of my oversensitive skin, does he start to move up my body.

Licking, sucking and biting his way as his hands pull the material of my shirt up. His hands wrap around my back and lift me slightly as he fingers the clasp on my bra. When it gives, he makes quick work of continuing his journey of hands and mouth until his teeth bite down on my right nipple.

The feeling of pleasurable pain makes me jolt and he gruffs out a laugh against my skin.

He takes his time rolling each of my nipples against his tongue. Nibbling softly and biting down hard as I arch and writhe under his touch.

"Thought about nothing but this for months, Megan. Since the last time I had your pussy choking my cock, this has been running through my mind. I wanted to take my time, go slow, make it good, but there will be nothing slow about this time, darlin'," he says against my breast.

I say nothing, but squeak when his hands push under my pits and push me further back in his bed, allowing him the room to drop his knee between us.

"I need to fuck you, hard."

"Please," I answer.

"When you come, you scream my name. When you called me Lee, fuck baby, felt it squeeze my balls so tight I could have come in my pants. Dig those heels in my spine, your nails in my shoulder, and you. Call. Me. Lee."

I gasp and try to nod. His eyes search mine for a beat and then he lifts, reaches over to the side of his bed and I watch as he rips a condom open and rolls the latex down his shaft.

When he's done, his hands move until he's holding me with

his fingers wrapped around my neck and his thumbs resting against my throat.

"I didn't want to give you an angry come, but it's been building for months. Building so high until that's all I can give you. Next time, you ride me until you take what you need. Put me in you, darlin'," he grunts.

I reach with an unsteady hand, between our bodies, and take his cock in my hand, running my fingers over the condom-covered skin until he groans.

"Now," he demands and I stop teasing and move the tip of him where my body is weeping to be filled.

"Fuck," he grinds out, his eyes never leaving mine.

His hands tighten slightly, not in a painful way, but the pressure against my throat makes me whimper just the same. The feeling of him holding me there while his body is heavy against mine works to have me climbing the high as my orgasm threatens again. And as he fills me in a bruising thrust that has the sound of his balls hitting my wet skin echoing out around us, my mouth drops and I cry out.

"You're soaking me, Megan. You want it harder?" he grunts against my lips.

I push my head up, his hands tighten against my throat and I feel another gush leave my body.

"Fucking love it when I'm rough? God, your pussy is so greedy for me. Just me," he rambles and then crashes his mouth to mine.

His hips pound against mine and his mouth swallows each and every cry that leaves my mouth. He continues his bruising pace as his hands leave my neck, I instantly miss the pressure and let it be known with a low whine. He sucks my tongue in his mouth and dips one elbow in the mattress as his other hand glides down my body and up the leg that is wrapped tight around his back.

His mouth leaves mine and with his hand still on my leg, he demands, "Dig your heels in deep, baby."

I give him what he wants, but not because he told me to. I give him what he wants because when his hand leaves my leg and pushes into the mattress, bringing his body up he goes even deeper into my body and those heels push hard.

Just as he demanded earlier, my hands go to his shoulders on my own accord and as he takes my body hard, my nails dig in with my heels still pushing hard against the small of his back. Our eyes never leave each other's probing gaze. Never once do I take my eyes away from his, so full of lust that I know there isn't an ounce of control left in his body.

He drops his head and I lift up to meet him in a kiss so sweet it doesn't match the powerful way that he's taking my body. A kiss that gives me more than words ever could at this moment. His hips slow and as his tongue rolls against mine, his hips start to take me in slow, deep rolls. He doesn't pull back, just rocks his hips against mine.

I push up and cry out when he slips even deeper.

His lips come from mine and his hooded eyes open a sliver. "Feels like heaven," he says softly. "Everything, darlin'. Feels like everything."

He drops his head, his forehead, wet with sweat, and hits mine softly. Then he starts to move, slowly dragging his cock from my body before pushing back in even slower. Each thrust he takes, every pull back of his hips, bringing me closer to breaking into a million pieces.

My breath comes quickly, matching his pants above me. It's building so high that I know the power of my release is going to tear me in two.

"I feel it," I gasp. "I feel it, Lee."

"God, yes." His eyes close and he drops his body down so that he's resting on his elbows, arms pushed under my shoulders, and my head in his palms. "Finally."

I feel tears leak from my eyes at the beauty of this moment and while I'm wide open for him in every way that counts, I push back against his hold and when I come, it isn't Liam that I scream . . . it's Lee. And the reward of this moment is when this big beautiful man, closes his eyes on a hard exhale and whispers *my* name like it's the most precious thing he has ever experienced.

Chapter 16

Liam

WATCH AS MEGAN MOVES FROM my bathroom and walks through the dim lighting of my bedroom before her knee hits the mattress and she crawls up my body, before settling half on top of me and half on the bed. Her head hits my shoulder, her arm wrapping around my torso and her legs tangling with mine. She doesn't speak and I give her the silence she needs. Her body is completely relaxed against mine. I take a deep breath as her fingers start to move against my chest in small circles.

Each circle her fingers take has me wondering where her thoughts are running to. I don't worry because after what we just shared, I know there is no way she's going to pull away this time. She let me in and fuck if it wasn't the most beautiful thing I've ever experienced.

"My . . . Jack. Jack didn't love me. I know he didn't, but I was happy with him. He gave us a happy life."

My body goes solid at her words. The hand that had been resting lightly against her back jolting and pulling her tighter against me.

"He cared for me and he cared deeply, but it wasn't love. The only love we ever shared was what we had as friends. Best friends all our lives." She takes a shuddered breath before her hand continues the circles against my skin. "He protected me. Made my life safe. Gave up everything he had, even his life, for that safety. Even knowing all of that, looking at what we had, it feels like the lie that it was now. I remember the happiness. I remember never regretting the path our lives took. But, looking back, all I can focus on is how I didn't feel and a big part of that is the love we lacked as lovers. I hate feeling that. Hate it. It feels like I cheapened his life somehow."

"Darlin'," I start and try to move her so I can see her eyes.

"No. No, Lee. I need this," she says and pushes her body even closer.

I keep my mouth shut and wait. I know she's about to speak when those circles pick back up.

"I was seventeen when he managed to drag me to one of the parties the football team was famous for. He was my best friend and it hurt him that I was living a life full of nightmares. He wanted me to have fun. Get out of the house where my crackhead mom was passed out and my drunk of a father was doing his best job at drowning in a bottle. So I went, because I wanted to see what the big deal was. Why he had been begging me for so long to go with him. I figured what the hell, school was over the next week and we would finally be graduating. He would always say, 'Megs, it's a big world past this park.' Or 'Megs, you just need to live a little.' He always saw the best in everything. He could see past the crappy trailer park we lived. Past the terrible parents, through the poor status of our financial lives, over the glooming fact that no one in either of our families had made anything of themselves. So, for him, I went and tried to see what he saw."

My body feels like it has cement flowing through my veins. Turning me into stone as each muscle pulls tight, bracing for her words but not daring to move while she is finally giving me the rest of her.

"We had been there for a few hours before he left me to run and pee. He hadn't left my side once. Not because he felt like he had to stay, but because that's just the type of friends we were. He wanted to share his excitement with everything he did with me. He was the life of the party and I was not. But for those few hours I had actually had fun. I got him. When he left me, he told me not to move, but the second he mentioned the bathroom it was like the floodgates opened and I needed to go right that second. He went through the back door and straight into the woods behind the house, and I . . . and I went down the dark hall like the stupid little girl I was."

Her hand stops and I know she's lost in her memories.

I can see what's coming even without the words. In my line of work this is a scene we see. Not a lot but too often to sit right. But even knowing what's coming and being ready to hear it is two different things. I give her the only thing I can while I wait for those circles to continue against my skin. I tighten my hold and pull her as close against me as I can get.

And wait.

"Two guys I had never seen in my life got to me before I even got close to the bathroom. They were older, which wasn't rare with those parties, for some of the college kids from the local community college to show. Twenty minutes later what little innocence I had left was gone as they took turns stripping it from me. They were smart, took me down to the basement where there was one of those soundproof rooms. Apparently the kid who lived there, his dad was some hot shot in the record business. Had his own recording studio, locked so tight it didn't matter how hard I yelled for someone to save me. Jack found me. He missed them by seconds. I will never forget the look in his eyes as he picked me up and helped me leave the house without anyone seeing me. I know that cost him, taking care of me and not going after *them*. It cost him even more to keep that secret. One that no one, besides you now, him and those two men know."

"Darlin', please," I beg as a feeling of helplessness so strong takes hold.

"You need to know. I wish I could keep this from you, but I don't want to start this with my ghost pulling me down anymore."

I nod, my chin rolling softly against her head.

She shifts and her body moves from my side until she's draped across me completely. Her forearms rest against my chest and her tiny hands land on my face, her thumbs tracing my lips as she looks into my eyes.

"Molly isn't Jack's." Her voice, so small with those three

words and I hold her eyes and wait for her to finish.

Giving her what she needs. It kills me to keep quiet and let her voice her pain. Fucking guts me. She needs this and all I can do is wrap my arms around her and wait it out.

"I have no clue who her father is, Lee. No clue," she continues.

She closes her eyes and two tears roll down her cheeks. I bring my arms around from the hold I had on her and wipe them away, causing her to open her eyes again. I search her gaze and make sure she is holding strong. She gives me a small nod.

"After I was raped, I didn't even consider the possibility. I wasn't stupid, but I had been too busy healing the wounds they left on my soul that it didn't even filter through. When I found out I was pregnant, Jack took charge. He wouldn't listen to a word I said. He enlisted the next day and a week later we were married. He knew, God he knew, if he left me there I would rot. And, Lee, I would have. He gave up everything for me. He had a full ride playing football and he was so good. He gave it all up to marry his best friend because he felt responsible for what happened to me."

"Baby, he loved you," I tell her honestly.

She shakes her head and it kills me that she really believes that.

"Megan, look at me. *See me, darlin'.*" I plead. I wait for her to collect herself before I continue. "You know I love Dani like she's my sister. You and Jack are just like Dani and me. Best friends with a bond that can't be shaken. He didn't give up anything for you that he wasn't okay with losing. But he was not okay with losing you. He did what he did because he loved you. Have you been living with that guilt this whole time?"

"Since the day he told me he enlisted. He did it all for me, Lee and in the end he died for it. I've felt that every day for the last six years. He gave me a happy life, you have to understand that, we were so blissfully happy that I didn't mind that we had the most unconventional marriage. But I have always felt the guilt of his decision since the day when he made it. I didn't show him. Never let him see that cloud hanging over us, but it was there and I felt the bone-crippling pain of that guilt when they told me he was killed."

"You need to let that go, darlin'. Let go of that thought that he didn't love you and forget it. I'm telling you, as a man cut from the same cloth, if Dani had been in your shoes, I wouldn't have married her, baby. Not because I wouldn't have wanted her safe, but because I don't love her past a sibling-like bond. I would have made her safe, but not by marrying her. Your husband, baby, he loved you."

Her eyes widen and I watch, helplessly, as her lids fill and when the first sob hits her body, I take her in my arms and hold her as she not only relives her pain, but comes to terms with the realization that she's had it all wrong for six very long and very agonizing years.

"I didn't love him like that, Lee." She says a long while after the tears had dried and her body had stilled. "What kind of person does that make me, that I never loved him like that? He was my best friend and I loved him, but I was never ever in love with him. Not when he saved me, made it safe, or even after we had Molly and we fell into a real marriage. It always felt so forced when we tried to be more than just friends."

I tighten my arms and close my eyes. I run my fingers through her hair before resting my hand against her head as it rests against my chest.

"Makes you human, Megan. You two made the best out of a shit situation. He died serving his country, baby. He died a hero. He died knowing he was a father of a beautiful girl that has her mother's smile and the fighting spirit of the only real father she will ever know—your husband. He loved a good woman and if I had my guess, with all of that, he died happy. Darlin', it's time to let it go. Give it to me and let me take your pain, but you never forget that despite everything that happened before, he loved you and Molly, and he died a happy man that had the world."

"How do you know that?" she sobs, her tears picking back up. Tears she needs to finally heal from her pain. Tears that, as they soak through my naked skin, heal because I take her pain.

"Because, there is no way he could have you and Molly in his life and not know what kind of beauty he held in his hands. Darlin' trust me. He didn't regret a second of it. Bet my life on it."

"Oh, God," she sobs. "Lee."

My name comes out of her mouth and I know that I will never forget the sound. Her agony laced so deep into that one word that long into the night I hold her to me, tight, as she slips in and out of sleep. The tears don't leave for long and even when she managed to drift off to sleep, those sobs never stop shaking her body.

My hold never wavers as I make true to my promise and take every single pain filled tear, every ghost of her past that comes shaking from the force of her cries, and I pull that pain deep inside and lock it tight so that it can never hurt her again.

Chapter 17

Megan

"**G**OOD MORNIN,' DARLIN'."

I shake my head against his voice and burrow deeper into his warm skin.

"I would let you sleep the day away if I could. No place I would rather have you than right here naked in my arms, but we need to talk and I want some time to enjoy my woman, soft from sleep, before we have to get going."

Lifting my head, I look through the blonde mess of hair that is currently more in my face than his now. His eyes look tired, but alert. The stubble from last night has darkened his jaw even more, framing that knee-melting smile to perfection.

"You need to use the restroom before we have that talk?" he asks, that smile deepening until his dimple pops.

I nod and before he unwraps his arms from my body, his head

tips up from the pillow it was resting on and his lips touch mine. So soft it was just a breath of his skin before he pulled away.

"Hurry back to me, darlin'."

Without too much fanfare, I untangle my body from his, instantly missing the warmth of his touch. I hear him laugh as I pull the sheet with me as I stand and I turn to glare at him, but stumble on my feet instantly. My glare vanishes and my jaw drops.

I should have considered, possibly, that it wasn't the best idea to take the only sheet we had with me. All I thought was that there was no way I wanted to parade through his very bright bedroom with all my jiggly bits on display. But, I didn't think because in nabbing that sheet, I left him—all of him—on display and he's loving every second of this. Very obviously.

My eyes go from his erection to his face a few times, not stopping to enjoy the deliciousness in between. Just like a tennis match, crotch to head and back again. My eyes widen when his laughter picks up and that beautifully huge erection of his bobs up and down. Just jumping around like a Mexican jumping bean or something. There wasn't any going back to his eyes after that. My gaze was trapped on his cock and it would take an act of God to change that.

"Keep looking at me like that and we're going to have issues," his voice grumbles.

I lick my lips and all his laughter stops. But my eyes never leave his crotch. Jesus, is he getting harder?

"Megan," he warns.

I don't move. My hands itch where I have the sheet clamped tight against my chest and I have to shift from foot to foot with the building pressure between my legs. He *is* getting harder.

"Lick your lips like that again and I won't be able to hold back."

His voice sounds strained. Well, hell, judging by how angry his cock looks, I would guess strained is a pretty fair assumption.

"Megan," he barks and I jump slightly. "Bathroom. Now. We need to talk before I fuck you and if you keep this shit up there won't be any of the former. Just a lot of fucking."

I nod then lick my lips. When I hear him make some kind of animalistic noise deep in his throat, I jump, spin and run to the bathroom.

I make quick work of the toilet, wash my hands and attempt to do something with my wild hair. When I look at myself in the mirror I want to puke. My eyes are swollen from crying most of the night; little, puffy red bags making them look small and beady. My nose is red and my lips are slightly chapped.

I look like a hot mess.

And Liam—no Lee—still wanted me. A lot.

I smile to myself when I think about what calling him Lee does to him. The second I used his nickname, something I have never done because I felt like by not using it I could keep some more distance between us, he came alive and the reward was so great that there is no way I'm going back to Liam.

My gaze falls from my face and I look around the counter. I see his toothbrush resting in a cup next to the sink. The toothpaste on the other side, neatly capped and not a mess like some people leave theirs. A girly looking bottle of hand soap, that I know deep down either came from his mom or Dani. No way he would have something like that. Lee strikes me as the kind of man that would have a bar of off brand soap, but not high-end girly stuff.

Shifting on my feet, I worry my lip and try to figure out the whole smelly breath, yucky teeth, situation I have myself in right now.

"Megan," Lee barks from the other side of the door. "Did you fall in?"

I take a deep breath, hike the sheet tighter and turn to open the door. He hasn't moved from his bed, his hands folded behind his head and that gloriously hard cock still standing at full attention.

"Stop," he warns and my eyes shoot to his. He studies my face for a second before speaking. "What's bothering you, darlin'." His tone is soft, comforting.

He starts to come up, his elbow digging into the mattress as his feet uncross and he starts to swing his frame from where he had been resting. I hold my hand up and he pauses.

"I, uh, well . . . okay. I know you're a single guy living alone and all, but sometimes single guys stock up and like to be prepared. I mean, I'm prepared, but I have Molly so it makes sense to have, like, ten of everything—"

I snap my mouth shut when he lifts off the bed and prowls toward me. He moved so quickly that one second he was in the bed, and the next he was standing in front of me with his hands resting right where my back meets the swell of my ass.

"Breathe,"

I do and he smiles.

"Not single," he states and I feel my brow wrinkle. "Darlin', wasn't alone in that bed last night. I. Am not. Single."

"Oh," I say on a sigh.

"Darlin'." He dips his neck down and moves his face level with mine. "Seriously?"

I shiver with the look in his eyes. Soft and hard, all at the same time. But not for a second holding back his happy adoration.

"Seriously?" he questions again.

Coming out of my fog, I shake my head and when he pulls back I hurry to find my voice.

"I know," I gasp. "I know. I mean, I think I know. I, you, uh . . . we . . . what I mean is, shit. I just wanted to know if you have a spare toothbrush."

I look up when I feel his body start to move slightly and his knee-melting smile hits me at full force, dimple and all.

"It isn't funny, Lee."

His eyes drop with my words and those hands at my lower back move down and hit my bottom. With each hand, his fingers flex and he pulls me closer. I stumble when the sheet tangles with my feet, but move to fall into his body. My eyes losing his as my vision fills with his tan chest.

"You aren't single either, Megan."

"I just need a toothbrush," I mumble against his skin and pull back enough to place a kiss against his pec.

"And you know you aren't single."

"I know," I whisper.

"You know that because last night, you felt it. You felt *every-thing* that I've seen since day one."

I nod, but don't speak.

"You felt it all."

"I did," I confirm and with my words, I take the last bit of the wall I had around me for years and kick the shit out of it. "Lee, I just need a toothbrush."

His body shakes, hard this time, and I pull my head back just in time to see him tip his head back and laugh. The sound, rich and like velvet to my skin, brings a smile to my face and a feeling of completeness settles in, taking the void I have felt for so long and filling it so full, it's spilling over the edge.

"Had my mouth on you just hours ago. All over you, darlin'. My mouth was inside of you. As deep as I could go. I think it's safe to say, my toothbrush, is your toothbrush."

I narrow my eyes and his smile grows.

"You just ruined the moment, bucko!" I snap and pull from his body then stomp into the bathroom.

His laughter trailing behind me.

And when I look in the mirror for the second time this morning, I don't see that lingering sadness. I pick up his toothbrush and as I stand there and brush my teeth, all I see is happiness.

Finally.

I unloaded on him last night and I know he wants to talk about that, I just don't know what to say. It was so much easier in the darkness. I used his strength and that helped to get the courage to open up. He deserves me giving it all to him and in order to do that I need to give him the light too.

With a deep breath of courage, I rinse off his brush and open the door. He walks over from the spot just in front of the door where I left him, the second I step out of the bathroom. His head comes down and I get a quick kiss.

"Don't get dressed, darlin'. I like your skin on mine."

And then he's gone, with the bathroom shutting to a crack behind him.

Well.

I might not get dressed, but the sheet stays.

My ass had just hit the bed when he came back into the room. Not even giving one thought to the fact that he is *still* very naked and very aroused. I hear his laugh and snap my eyes up from where I had, once again, been staring at his erection.

"Darlin' I really need you to focus. You'll get my cock when we finish, okay?"

"I am focusing," I retort.

He laughs, "Yeah, focusing on my cock isn't going to help us right now."

He reaches out and his large hand wraps around the base of his shaft. His long fingers curling to pull his sac up. He moves his hand, fingers dropping his sac, and he gives himself a few lazy pulls. I close my eyes and drop my body to fall to the mattress with a groan.

I feel the mattress dip with his weight and when my eyes open his face is right there, so close that our noses are just a breath away.

"Good morning, darlin'," he says, repeating those words he rumbled earlier.

So carefree and confident. He's changing me. Every second that I'm with him, I feel myself changing into a person that feels the lightness of happiness. *He* is making me a better person.

"Hey," I smile.

His hand moves up my side and when he reaches the top of the sheet, it's pulled and thrown away from our bodies and out of my grasp in seconds.

"I told you, I like your skin on mine."

My pulse speeds up and I look into his amused eyes.

"You have nothing to hide from me, Megan. Not your body and not your thoughts."

"Okay," I gulp.

"We need to talk, darlin'," he tells me softly, his eyes searching.

"I know."

"Do you want me to start?"

I nod and he gives me a quick kiss before adjusting our bodies. When he's done, my back is to the mattress and his large body is covering mine. He keeps his weight off, but still manages to make me feel like I'm covered head to toe in his strength. Our legs are tangled together, his body turned slightly so that, even with me fully in his arms, his hips are on the bed next to me. One of his arms goes under my body at my shoulders and the other hits right under my chest, his long fingers wrapping around the base of my breast. His face dips into my neck and he gives me a kiss before pulling back and looking into my eyes.

"You gave me a lot of heaviness last night. Pain that you've carried for a long time, darlin', and I know that has to leave you hurting. Honesty here, complete honesty, it cut me to the bone to hear what's been weighing you down for years, Megan. It's a pain I don't mind, if it means you've unloaded some of that weight for me to carry. What I need is to know where your head is."

He waits, his unwavering patience with me so clear in this moment.

"It's gone," I whisper, my eyes never leaving his.

"What is, baby?"

"The pain."

His eyes close and the arms holding me go tight.

"I have a lot of years thinking one way, that won't go away over night, but what you said, about Jack, hearing that and letting those thoughts roll through my head all night . . . you're right. Every memory I have of him, before and after Molly, there isn't one that he isn't over the moon happy. Even though we didn't share a love that was built conventionally, I can see it now. He was my best friend and he made my life a better place as a child and as my husband."

"He held the world, darlin', no doubt in my mind about how he felt."

"He would love you."

"Yeah?"

He settles and I roll slightly so that I'm about to look into his eyes, our bodies now facing each other.

"It's hard, because I will always miss him and I would never wish Molly away, but had my life taken a different turn and I met you . . . he would have been our biggest cheerleader." Reaching up, my hand cups his jaw. "He always wanted me to live a life better than what we were born into. He saw it for himself, but I couldn't, not for the life of me, see beauty coming from that. He would joke that one day I would walk right into a new life and I would be too busy living in my head that I would miss it until my ass hit the ground. Lee, you pack a mean punch and I think my ass still feels the sting of the ground."

"You see it now, huh?" He looks deep into my eyes and blinds me with that smile.

"Yeah, baby, I see it. I see everything that I couldn't see before. Everything."

"I won't let you go, Megan. I waited and I knew the second that I saw you that this was it for me. Do you know how hard it was to keep my distance and wait for you to be ready?"

"I'm still scared," I tell him honestly.

His body moves closer and I move into his body until my arms wrap around us and I feel him completely.

"You get that what I had with Jack was something that, when I lost him, almost destroyed me?" He nods and I continue in hushed tones. "That almost destroyed me and the way I feel toward you, even this early, I know it's so much more powerful."

"It's not early, Megan. I've been here, picking away at your walls for almost two years." He laughs but it holds no humor. "If it hadn't been Dani and Cohen's wedding, it would have happened not long after. You were weakening around me every time I was near and it was only a matter of time. We've spent enough time together that you know what you feel. It's never too soon when you're sure. We didn't just meet on the streets. We've been building this for a long while, darlin'."

"That doesn't mean I'm not scared, Lee."

"I know, but we'll get there. Together. You just have to take my hand and let me take care of your heart."

I nod, not trusting my voice right now.

"Almost done. Can you handle more?"

"I'm okay, Lee. I really am. Last night was hard, but I feel free of that pain. It just stings a little."

"First, before we finish this up. You need to know that you never have to keep Jack from me. You shared a life with him and he's a part of you and a part of Molly. I want you to be able to come to me and know that I will never, not once, turn you away. He gave you a good life, baby, and he should never be kept in the dark."

My eyes fill with tears and I nod, my hands flexing against the skin on his chest. I move them around his back and hug myself to his body.

"Thank you for that," I tell him.

"You don't have to thank me, darlin'," his voice rumbles against my ear. "I don't want to bring this back up. It kills me, but I have to know so that I don't fuck something up unintentionally. Is Jack on Molly's birth certificate?"

"Uh, yeah." I tell him, confusion with the path this conversation has turned.

"I assume that means that you two decided before she was born there would be a certain amount of care when it comes to Molly's knowledge of how she was conceived?"

"She will never know. Never, Lee. I don't ever want that to darken her life. Ever."

He must have read the panic in my tone because his body moves until he's sitting, back to the headboard, my legs spread wide framing his thighs, until he's settled his arms back around me. His hands squeeze my hips before moving up to curl around my neck.

"She can't know," I gasp.

"And she won't, Megan. You trusted me with that last night and I will never betray that. I needed to know so that I could proceed with a full deck. She was and will always be Jack's, okay?"

I study his face. Those eyes giving me nothing but understanding and I nod.

"You're mine now, darlin', and with that comes Molly. It's a package deal that I want more than you'll ever know. This is up to you on how we play this, but she knows me. That little girl stole my heart the first time she put hot pink lipstick on me, so it isn't going to be a hardship for me here, but I need to know how you want to introduce *us* to her."

This is it. This step will be me giving myself over to him completely and with a newfound strength, I give it to him.

"She's young, but not stupid. I'll talk to her when I pick her up. Give her some time to hear it from me before. I saw her with you, Lee, I know this will not be news that isn't exciting for her. But I don't want to throw us in her face. We start with dinner. Then we take it as it comes. Together."

"I like that, darlin'."

His lips hit mine in a deep kiss that holds the promise of more before he pulls back.

"Thank you," he tells me.

"For what?"

"Everything."

Then I get his lips.

And then he gives *me* everything.

Chapter 18

Liam

I LOOK OVER AT MEGAN AS we drive toward her house. She called to check on Molly right before we left, letting Izzy know that she would be there to get her shortly after lunch. That gave us two hours to fill and I used every second of our time until we had to leave. After last night I've been worried that she would be having a hard time, but she's shown no signs that the pain she held onto for so long is haunting her.

She's lighter.

Her laughter coming easier and her lips have been curved up since I pulled her from the bed and into the shower.

I can tell she's holding back a little, that fear of starting something new won't go away overnight, but she's ready.

And she's finally mine.

"How do you think this is going to go?"

She turns her gaze from the window and gives me her eyes. I get a smile before turning my focus back to the road ahead of us.

"Molly?" she asks.

"Yeah, darlin'."

That smile grows. I can't see it fully, but even while my eyes are on the road I can hear it in her voice.

"She won't even blink."

I laugh, "Meaning?"

"Molly loves easy and hard. She is happy when I'm happy. She enjoys life with a full speed ahead attitude. My guess is that she's going to be riding the high of me telling her you're going to be around, a lot, for a long while to come."

"She's a great kid," I voice honestly.

"Yeah," she sighs.

I reach over and pull her hand over the console and hold it against my lap.

"I won't make you regret this, giving us a chance. I promise you that I will do everything in my power to drive the three of us on this new path."

Her hand squeezes mine.

"I know, Lee. For the first time in a really, really long time I'm excited to see what happens next."

We continue the drive in silence as I hold her hand in my lap.

When I pull up to her house and I watch as she hesitates to leave my truck, I grin and climb out to walk over to her door. She gets down and I laugh to myself as she visibly has to force herself to leave me.

When we get to her door, I pull her into my arms. She doesn't hesitate to wrap her arms tightly around my back.

"I'll be back tonight, darlin'. If you think that Molly isn't ready for that, you call and we will try tomorrow."

"Okay."

"You're going to have to walk through that door, baby. If I had my way I wouldn't let you go, but one step at a time."

"Okay," she says into my chest.

"Give me a kiss," I demand.

Her head comes up, "Okay, Lee."

When her lips touch mine, that smile never slips.

"See you tonight."

She nods and I wait for her to unlock her door, getting another grin before she shuts the door. I stand there for a second before I walk back to my truck and pull out of her driveway.

I've been ready for this moment for what seems like a lifetime and now that I have it, I'm nervous as hell. Not for what I'm building with Megan, but with the unknown that Molly is. She's been through so much in her short life that I don't want to rush my presence in her life. I don't want her to feel like I'm taking her father's place either. In all the times that I've been around her while Dani was watching her, she didn't even blink around the men that came around. Nate and Zac had often sat in on our tea parties and she ate that attention up.

But, there's a big difference between playtime while she's with Dani and a man being in her everyday life.

In all my plans to make Megan mine, I never doubted a single step. I never feared that it wouldn't work and I was never nervous.

Funny that all it takes is one five-year-old girl to have me breaking out in a sweat.

My thoughts are interrupted when my phone's ringer starts coming through the truck speakers. Looking at the display in my dash, I see Dani's name come up.

"Hey," I answer.

"She just called Mom to tell her she would be there in thirty minutes to get Molly. Mom called me to let me know that. Now I know she isn't with you . . . so spill!"

"You get that I have a dick and gossip sessions don't apply to me, right?"

"Shut the hell up and tell me!" she huffs.

I flick my blinker and head toward my house while I process my thoughts and for the first time, I don't tell Dani everything. My promise to Megan and the relationship we're building means more to me than anything else in my life. Even the best friend that knows every single thing about me.

"I'm having dinner with her and Molly tonight."

"Uh," she falters. "Is that it?"

"That's all you're going to get."

"Seriously?" she gasps.

"Love you, Dani, but last night Megan finally, thank Christ, broke through the chains that have been holding her captive and those moments are for her and me alone."

"Oh my God," she wheezes. "That is so beautiful."

I roll my eyes.

"If she lets you in, then good. I'll be happy with the outcome either way because right now I know she's moving on and we're going to do that together. It's good, Dani. Really good."

"I'm so happy for you, Lee."

"Thanks, babe."

"How do you feel about tonight? Nervous? You are, aren't you?"

"Dani, I'm out of my mind, could puke, nervous."

She laughs and proceeds to spend the rest of my ride home talking my nerves down.

Chapter 19

Megan

I'M GOING TO PUKE.

Maybe.

Probably.

"Is he here yet, Mommy?"

"Not yet, little bird," I tell Molly and laugh when her little lips pull into a frown.

To say my daughter is excited would be a great understatement.

"Come here, baby. He'll be here soon and then you can tell him all about our day."

She climbs into my lap and settles in to wait. Sofia the First fills the room and I settle back with her curled against me and think about how the morning went.

It wasn't the same madness that had met me the last time I

picked her up from the Reid's. Since I didn't arrive until well after lunch—thanks to a very long shower with Lee—Axel had already left for work, dragging Nate with him to 'learn the ropes,' according to a laughing Izzy. I think Izzy could tell my nerves were sparked bright. Her knowing eyes spoke volumes. Of course, she also knew that I spent the night with Lee since the first words I stuttered were just that.

"I think Lee is my boyfriend," I told her with my cheeks flaming.

Izzy had barked out a laugh and pulled me into a tight hug.

"That's just their way, honey. His father was the same way with Dee. Axel the same with me. Greg and Melissa. Maddox and Emmy. Asher and Chelcie. My sweet Dani with Cohen. Heck, even Davey had his moment with Sway. These men, it's just how they are. When they set their minds to something there is nothing and no one that will hold them back. And sweetheart, before you even let this thought take root in your mind, when they know, they know and they know in a way that sticks forever."

Of course *that* did nothing but make me freak out even further, causing Izzy to laugh harder, and Molly to join in while dancing in circles around us. I came down from my freak out . . . until I got my little bird home and while I watched her pick and peck at her snack, my nerves climbed once again.

I should have known better. With Molly, there needed to be no doubt.

Leaning my head back, I settle in for our wait and playback my conversation with Molly.

"Mommy, what did Mrs. Izzy mean? About being sticky for-

ever?"

I turn my head from the counter I had been wiping—the same spot for the last five minutes—while staring off into space. Her brown eyes full of curiosity smile up at me from the table.

"Not sticky forever, little bird. She was talking about a feeling, kind of. She meant it like how I love you will be a feeling that sticks to me like yummy, chewed up bubble gum."

Her nose crinkles and her lips twist in a way that I know she's holding in a giggle. "That's gross, Mommy!" she tells me seconds before peals of laughter come bubbling out of her mouth. "I don't want to stick to you with chewy bubblegum!"

Smiling, I move from the counter and over to sit next to my sweet, full-of-love, daughter.

"It's a little different than that, sweets, that's just the best way to explain it."

She stops laughing out loud, but those eyes of hers are still burning with amusement. I watch her expressive face as she thinks about what Izzy told me and what I just told her. And then I watch as all of it plugs into the right plugs and the connection is made.

"Who do you want to stick to with chewy bubblegum, Mommy?"

Ah, my smart little bird. She's always been so wise beyond her five small years.

"I don't want to stick to anyone with yucky, chewy bubblegum," I laugh.

Her small hand comes out and falls on top of where I have mine placed on the table. Small thumb rubbing and little pink tipped nails going up and down in a thoughtful wave as she looks at me.

"Yes you do."

"No, baby. Just you."

"You're silly, mommy bird!"

"And you're sillier, little bird."

Her fingers continue their light thumping against my skin and I watch her eyes get soft and full of love, all for me.

"You told Mrs. Izzy that Leelee is your boyfriend. Is he the one you want to stick to with chewy bubblegum?"

Ah.

There it is.

My opening to tell her.

And my opening for a spiked up, nerve filled, freak out.

I went over this a million times since Lee left and I picked up Molly. How much to tell her. How to tell her. Is it too soon? How she would feel. Every possible thought of fear, followed by excitement, and then back to fear mixed with worry.

But my little bird is smart. Smart and knowing. And more importantly, I owe it to her to be honest about our future.

A future that I hope to God will be filled with Lee.

"I wouldn't want to be stuck to him with chewy bubblegum, but yes, sweets, I would very much love to be stuck with him."

"Like that time my arms got stuck in my swim wings? When you couldn't get them off?"

My smile grew as some of those nerves let go of their strong hold. "Something like that, little bird."

"Will Leelee come over for tea parties now?"

"Yeah, baby, I think so."

"Will Leelee make you smile all the time?"

Oh. My. God.

"You make me smile all the time."

Her head tilts and she smiles a smile that is so small you almost can't tell it's there. It's a sad smile. One that I know—and hate—that I've put on her face.

"Not all the time. You don't smile all the time."

"Oh, baby. Come here."

She makes quick work of pulling out from the table and into my lap. I wrap my arms around her and hold her as tight as she's holding me.

"Mommy was sad for a long time, little bird. I'm so sorry for that. For not smiling all the time. I missed your daddy a lot and for a long time my missing him was too hard to smile."

"You smile a lot now," she mumbles into my chest.

"Yeah, sweets, I do."

"Does that mean you don't miss Daddy?"

I tighten my embrace before moving my hands under her arms and moving her body so that she can see my eyes.

"No, honey. I miss your daddy a lot and I always will, but the way I miss him is different than it was then. When he went to heaven, I missed him so much that all I could see was how much I missed him. I got lost for a while, baby, and I couldn't remember the way. You gave me my smiles, smiles so bright that you helped me light up the way then and you still do, but for a long time all I could see was your smiles but not the way they wanted me to go. Those smiles made me happy even though I missed your daddy and because I missed your daddy so much, I thought a lot of sad

things for a long time. But, now Mommy can see again. I can see my way that I had lost for a little while and, little bird, it's a beautiful path, so full of beautiful flowers, rainbows, and blue skies forever and ever. Now I can hold your hand and we can run through the flowers together. But, even while we run we can still miss Daddy. We just miss him in a different way."

"That sounds nice, Mommy."

"Yeah, honey, really nice."

"Will Leelee be with us when we run through flowers?"

My smile grows and I look into her very hopeful gaze and with a lightness I haven't ever felt in all of my years, I tell her, "Yes, Molly. He's going to come and run with us through the flowers and we're going to chew bubblegum and be stuck forever."

Her eyes light up and her face is the picture of joy.

"And we can have lots and lots of tea parties and make-upovers when we run in the flowers!"

After our talk, she went back to her snack and talked about Lee all afternoon. I let her know that he would be over for dinner later and I didn't think she would ever come down from that high.

Which brings us to now. My daughter, so full of eagerness over the night, that even with her favorite show on television, her eyes are glued to the hallway that leads to the front door.

I look at the clock, for the hundredth time in seconds, just as the front door thumps and the bell echoes through the house.

Molly's head snaps up and with wide, happy, eyes whispers, "He's here," before scampering off my lap, elbowing me—twice—in the ribs, and running as fast as her little legs will take her to the door.

"Molly, don't open that door until I'm there!" I yell, coming off the couch quickly.

"Too late," I hear and my nerves flutter like a million butterflies in my gut, rooting me in place.

"Mommy! Mommy! Leelee is here . . . and, and . . . and HE HAS FLOWERS!"

A head to toe tingle starts taking over my body. My lips curve and I move forward with the largest beaming grin on my face.

I walk forward and around the wall that separates the living room from the front door and stop dead at the sight that meets me.

Lee is holding my daughter in his strong arms while her face—bright with the happiness she is feeling—is stuffed into a small bundle of light pink roses. I look from her with wonderment to Lee's arm that isn't holding her tight to see another bundle—this one much larger—of more roses.

I don't move.

His brow tips up and I know he's wondering if he overstepped. This big, confident man that has gone after me with steadfast determination, is actually unsure and that has my feet moving before I can even process a single move I make. When my body hits his, the force of which I clearly didn't process, he rocks back slightly before his arm comes up and wraps around my shoulders. I reach out and pull my arms around both him and Molly, then shove my head into his neck.

"If you brought bubblegum, I swear I'll cry right now," I mumble into his skin before both Molly and I laugh so hard he has no choice but to hold onto us both a little tighter.

Chapter 20

Liam

"SHE ASLEEP?"

Megan drops down to the couch and curls into my side.

"Yes, finally. However I'm pretty sure she isn't sleeping heavy since she is still riding her Lee high."

I laugh, "Lee high?"

She comes up with her elbow pressed to the back of the couch and her hand against my chest, "Yes! Apparently the 'Lee high' is just as intoxicating to her as it is to me. This isn't funny," she snaps when my head goes back and I laugh. Hard.

"Darlin' that's the funniest thing I've heard. Lee high," I chuckle.

"Whatever," she gripes, moving her body to rest against mine again.

"Give me your mouth, Megan. I've missed it."

She shivers against my side. Her head snaps up and without giving her a second to think, my mouth comes down and I take her lips.

Just like I've been craving to do since she turned the corner earlier and stopped dead. But I wasn't worried because she had an expression on her face that I've been waiting to see.

The pain wasn't there anymore.

Not a single sliver of it had a hold on her beautiful body.

The weight of the world, off her shoulders, and even through her shock I could tell that she was . . . happy.

Bringing my hand up, I push my fingers into the silky hair on her nape and turn her head slightly so that I can deepen the kiss. Her tongue comes out, slowly, and slides against mine. Her head tilts and even though she doesn't move past her hands curling into my side and chest, with just one swipe of her tongue against mine, the hunger in that kiss grows. My cock swells against my pants and I know I'm in serious danger of this kiss becoming out of control when I feel her scissor her legs together.

Fuck me.

My girl can kiss.

Pulling back slightly, not removing my lips from hers, I give her a few light pecks. Not only to bring her back down from the rush I hope to fuck is burning through her body too, but pray it's enough to squash the urge scorching my blood, to sink my cock deep into her body.

Fuck me.

"I can smell you and, darlin', I've never thought it would be possible to want you more than I already do. Fuck, I crave you, Megan."

"Oh, God," she sighs and those damn legs start moving against each other again.

"I want nothing more than to lay you down, strip you bare, and worship every delicious inch, but that isn't happening tonight. I have no doubt this will cost me huge, but not tonight."

Her head comes down and crashes into my neck and I feel her nod.

"When Molly is used to me being around. When the excitement isn't so new and we know she's handling us, handling the knowledge that I will *not* be going anywhere, then we play. But until then, we wait until she isn't just a room away."

She nods again and her fingers curl even tighter, letting me know that I'm not the only one that is suffering right now.

"I need you to stop rubbing your thighs together, darlin'. Fuck me."

Her body shakes and when she pulls her head from my neck, her lips pulled in and I can tell she's about to lose her hold on her laughter.

"You have no idea how bad I want to fuck you, Megan," I tell her in a tone that came out harsher than I meant.

"I'm sorry," she says, laughter leaving her face.

Pulling her tighter to me, I press my lips to her temple. "Don't be sorry for wanting me. Don't ever be sorry for that, darlin'. You just have no idea how small that thread of my control is right now and as much as I crave your sweet body, we both know it can't happen."

"I know, Lee."

And fuck me if that doesn't go straight to my cock too.

Trying to think of a way to distract my need to fuck her, I ask, "Want to tell me why you and Molly both about lost your mind at the mention of gum earlier? I swear I thought I was going to go down, you two were laughing so hard."

"You're our gum," she bizarrely tells me.

"I'm not real good at understanding code, darlin'."

I move my arm when she pushes up and wait for her to settle. Instead of doing that at my side, one long leg comes up and settles at the opposite hip of her other. Her ass lands mid-thigh and both of her hands come up to my neck, curling around and then she leans in. Her face just inches from my own. I reach out and settle my hands to her hips and wait for her to speak. Enjoying the way she feels in my arms like this a little too much and vow to have her riding my cock like this real soon.

Her voice brings me out of my thoughts and I look into her eyes as she speaks.

"You, Lee. You are the chewy, icky, sticky, bubblegum that will never come off."

"Still not following, baby," I mutter against her lips.

"Well, I guess you aren't the gum. More like the one I want to stick the gum to. Or whatever. It makes a lot more sense when it comes from a five-year-old."

"Yeah, I'm guessing it does," I laugh. "Care to add on to that a little?"

Her head tilts in the most adorable way.

"Please," I try, earning me a curl of her small nose.

"It's really nothing. Actually it is nothing. It's silly. Just something that Izzy had said and Molly heard, then of course I explained in kid terms. So, I don't think it really makes sense, you know, to a man and all, if I explain it like I did to Molly."

If I thought her actions were cute before, this stuttering and rambling version of her takes the cake.

"It's kind of embarrassing," she tells me.

"I've been inside you. What I mean," I rush to finish when her eyes narrow, "Is that I've seen every inch. Touched, licked and kissed those inches. There is not one thing you should ever feel embarrassed about with me, Megan."

"Oh," she breathes.

"Yeah. Give it to me, baby."

And she does. God, does she. And in that moment I make a note to make sure Izzy Reid gets one hell of a thank you delivery of flowers.

"I might have been a little nervous this morning and blurted out to Izzy that I thought . . . that maybe you had . . . shit, okay, it just slipped out that you were maybe my boyfriend. Or had made me your girlfriend. But now, saying that out loud and to your face makes it sound kind of silly. Boyfriend and girlfriend, I mean. The label, that is."

I smile and she drops her head to mine.

"I told you it was embarrassing," she exhales.

"No, it isn't. The rambling you do when you're nervous is cute, darlin', that's all. So cute that it hits me right between my legs, so I would say that isn't embarrassing at all. I'm not huge on labels, but if that's what you need to know you're mine and I'm yours, then they work for me."

"Oh, okay," she says with red cheeks.

"God, you're cute."

Her lips curl and I pull my head from the back of the couch to give her a kiss, not deep, but I still feel it just the same and I'm fighting the urge once again to take her.

"And when did bubblegum come into play?" I ask.

"Right," she breathes. "So Izzy may have told me that you guys—all of you guys—have a history of this."

I feel my brows pull in and wait, not sure about where this is going.

"I mean . . . this is kind of hard to explain, but she kind of said that all of the guys, your dad, Axel, and all the way down to Cohen, have a way about making someone yours. A way that, when it happens, sticks forever. Molly was curious, having heard that, but not understanding everything else, and asked what it meant to be stuck together forever. So, I told her it was like bubblegum."

I nod, loving everything she's said, but still not getting the damn gum.

"Right. So, the best way to explain it to her was to tell her how being stuck together or wanting to be stuck together is a feeling and not really being stuck, but if it wasn't just a feeling, it would be like wanting to have someone as close as possible and that feeling is like being stuck with chewy, sticky bubblegum."

"Bubblegum," I mumble and she closes her eyes.

"Bubblegum," she echoes.

"Open your eyes, Megan."

She doesn't move.

"Darlin', see me."

And those brown eyes hit mine.

"I've got a brand new pack of spearmint in the truck. Happy as fuck that you would gladly use it to stick yourself to me, but you don't need the gum. I'm happily stuck and have no plans to become unstuck."

Her eyes shine and then her head goes back and her laughter hits me like a punch in the gut.

Perfection.

Her happy in my arms, her daughter safe and warm—also happy—in her bed, having the chance at something I've known would feel like this, has my hands pushed into her hair and her mouth on mine in seconds.

Only now I have a hard time reminding myself why I need to pull back before I get too lost in her.

Bubblegum, I think to myself as her tongue slides against mine and the mint taste I tasted earlier invades. One that only a slice of gum can leave behind.

I've never loved bubblegum more.

Chapter 21

Megan

M Y BODY IS GOING TO burn up from the inside if he keeps this up. These slow kisses that I know will not go a step further with Molly home, boiling my arousal so bright that my veins are on fire.

"You taste good," he mumbles against my neck.

"Bubblegum," I wheeze out when his teeth bite down on the sensitive skin between my neck and shoulder.

Then my brain catches up to my mouth when I lose his mouth and I feel his body move in amusement. My eyes open wide and I watch him attempt to stop his laughter, and fail.

"I'm never going to live that down."

His laughter dies down to a chuckle at my pouting tone.

"I'll probably never even be able to chew a piece again," I continue.

His chuckle stops, but his smile stays. His perfectly straight teeth bright against his tan skin.

"You probably think I'm nuts."

His smile doesn't slip as he shakes his head.

"I think I'm nuts."

His body starts to shake again and without a word, his mouth is back on mine. His tongue darting out to rub slowly against my closed lips until I give him the access he wants. Then he slides in and kisses me hard. So hard that all my thoughts of stupid bubble-gum leave instantly.

A while later, still in his arms watching *Pitch Perfect,* my choice not his, he breaks the comfortable silence we had slipped into after my bubblegum meltdown.

"I'm working tomorrow, pulling a double for another officer that needs the day to take his daughter on a school trip. That means I won't see you for a few days. The last double I pulled had me sleeping almost twenty-four hours straight. But, we need to finish the plans that got cut short—not that I mind one second of how they were cut short—but I still need to finish."

"Okay, Lee. You don't need to explain that to me."

"You get that we're together now?" he harshly asks.

"Uh, yeah."

"Then I need to explain that to you."

"I think, maybe, I should give you a little history of my life," I tell him, trying to not get annoyed with myself or more specifically the lack of experience I have when it comes to relationships. "I've been in a relationship with one man, Lee. And while I was married to him, what we shared wasn't a typical relationship. We were both faithful and while yes, we were intimate, it wasn't often. That being said, he didn't explain his plans for days to come with me. If he needed to do something, he would give us a kiss goodbye and go about his business. Before Jack, I didn't date. Not once. So, I think it would be a good guess that I'm about as stupid as it comes, when it comes to this," I point between him and myself. "I don't expect you to report to me."

His eyes go hard during my little speech and when I finish talking, I wait, bracing for him to realize what a mess I am and leave.

"It might not be tomorrow, or hell even a month from now, but you're going to fall into this relationship effortlessly. I know that because in the two days that we've established a togetherness, you've come out of your shell and without one doubt taken each step forward. I'm not telling you my plans for any other reason but for you to know while I may have to be somewhere else, I want to be here. I'm letting you know where I'll be because I *can't* be here, and trust me, I would rather be here than sitting in a patrol car for two ten-hour shifts. Give and take, darlin'. I'm giving you my plans so that when I don't, I can take."

"Take?" I question.

"The other night, when I took you to the clearing, I had planned for a night of four wheeling. Had my ATV out there waiting. No way in hell that I'm going to complain about how the night progressed, but I still have plans and those plans include that clearing, us and my ATV."

"Four wheeling"?

"Muddin', darlin'. We need to find another night after some

rain though. It was a perfect night to take the trails, but the second it rains we get a sitter for Molly and go."

"Okay, why would I want to do that?"

He laughs. "You'll see."

"That makes no sense, Lee. I've never been, but I know you end up dirty as all hell and I can't imagine the fun in riding around getting mud up my nose."

Small lie. I've heard Dani and the girls talk about all the times they've been off-roading. Sometimes they go in trucks, but often on ATVs. Each time they talk about them, I've stayed silent. Even though I'm curious, the thought of riding one of them without fear seems impossible to me. I've heard horror stories about people getting hurt and sometimes killed.

"It's a rush, Megan. It isn't about just driving around and splashing mud all over the place. You pick the right trail, hitting those climbs and knowing but not seeing what's coming has your body on one hell of a high. After a good rain, those trails are slippery and when you come over the climbs then race down to the waiting mud—it's all part of the rush. When that water and mud flies all over the place, I promise the last thing you will think about is that you're dirty and may or may not have mud in your nose."

"I still don't see the appeal here."

His face gets soft and I watch something move behind his eyes, gone too quickly for me to pinpoint. "How about you look at it this way. You'll be on the back of my machine while it rushes through the trails back on old man Sampson's property, your arms will be wrapped around my body. You will be pressed so tight to me that when the motor is rumbling and your hips move against mine, you will have to work real fucking hard not to think about how hard that is going to make me. And, darlin', when we're done, dirty and wet, I'm going to have a lot of fun cleaning you up."

"Oh. Well. I guess I could partake in a little off-road fun," I say, my voice hoarse with arousal.

Lee keeps his eyes on mine, the brown depths not hiding how turned on he is, and when a few minutes pass, he pulls me back into his arms and while looking at the television I hear, just barely, him mumble how 'cute' I am.

Lee's double shift ended up taking a lot more of his time than planned. He worked Monday for his shift and then the one he was covering, however he ended up having to take another one—with only two hours of sleep—when they called him back on. Apparently being understaffed is a huge issue for the HTPD. So huge of an issue that when two officers are down with a massive stomach virus, they have to call in one that's just come off a double.

Lee doesn't complain. He actually said he didn't mind going in, but was pissed that meant he would need to crash the second he finished his shift and wouldn't get to come over.

That was over a week ago and things have just been too crazy for us to get together. Between his work, my deadline, and Molly, there just hasn't been time to go out. That being said, our late night phone calls have kept me plenty entertained. If I thought Lee talking dirty in bed was hot, hearing his deep voice rumble over the phone, telling me everything he can't wait to do to my body, is unbelievable. Add to that the sounds of him coming when I return promises of my own has kept me aroused for eight very long days.

I pick up my cell and smile when I see Lee's text, reminding me that he'll be over tonight to pick me up for dinner. Actually, his reminder was that he was taking 'his' girls out and the mention of me and Molly being his girls has created a smile on my face that I'm pretty sure won't be slipping for a while.

Scrolling through my texts, I bring up Dani's and type out a new message.

Me: I need your help.

Dani: Shoot!

Me: Tonight is my first night out with Lee. I need to change some things up. It's time.

Dani: I've got a block empty around nine if you can get here in the next fifteen. I take it this is going to be more than just a cut?

I take a second and think about her question. I've been thinking about this since my quest to move on started. It's time, for me to let go of the old Megan and get a new look. Nothing crazy, but since I've had the same long blonde hair cut at regularly since I was a teen, yeah . . . it's time.

Me: It's for the new me.

Dani: Well, right on, babe! Sway is going to eat this up.

That man lives for makeovers.

Me: Uh.

Dani: Don't worry. This is going to be a blast! See you in fifteen.

Okay. So I guess I'm getting a makeover.

Chapter 22

Megan

SHOCK HOLDS ME IN PLACE as I'm being circled by Sway—the short, but fit, owner of the salon that Dani works at. He's probably a good three inches or so shorter than my five-foot-nine, however the five inch heels that he's rocking make him taller than I am. Not to mention, the man makes skinny jeans look better than I ever could. Of course, he doesn't have my hips. I've heard, but never seen, that he also rocks his long blond wig better than most women can.

Yeah, Sway is a force that you will only understand if you know him. He's flamboyant and over-dramatic, loves glitter to the degree that it is probably unhealthy, and isn't afraid to tell you exactly how it is.

He's also Stella's dad.

But even though I love Stella and even though Dani seems to

think this is a brilliant idea, having Sway circle me while mutter-
ing, is freaking me way out.

"Those hips, child! God, only the lucky ones have hips like
that. I've tried, trust me. I had hips when I was a sexy plump man,
but they never looked as good as yours. I bet that gorgeous man
just grabs hold and goes to town!"

My cheeks heat and I hear Stella, who also works at the salon,
yell at her dad to stop embarrassing me.

"Nothing to be embarrassed about. I've told you before,
child, I don't bat for the kitties but I still think like a man. Well,
sometimes. And those hips. Yes, honey . . . oh yes! Now come sit
in Sway's chair and tell me all about that hunk Liam Beckett."

Then my hand is in his and I'm being pulled past Dani and
into Sway's chair.

"You do realize she is my client, right?" she huffs.

"No. She was. Now she's mine."

I watch through the mirror as Dani puts her hands on her slim
hips and snaps, "You can't just steal my appointment. She's my
friend, you weird old man. I swear, if I didn't love you I would
quit."

He laughs, throwing his head back and his arms in the air.
"You," he points to her and then reaches out to unbutton the top
button on her black blouse, "Will never learn to let those babies
free. Can you believe her?" he asks, looking at me through the
mirror. "She has those great girls now that she's turned into a human milker. Never shows them off. I tell her, time and time again,
now that she has the man doesn't mean she should put them away.
And you," he snaps, turning back to Dani. "Leave me to this sweet

child. She needs Sway. You need to go tug up the girls and go give your man a nooner before he calls here, again, and yells at *me* for keeping you away from the house."

"He did not yell at you," she yells. "He just asked if I could take a longer lunch and then got a little upset when I had to leave before we finished."

"Oh yeah, and what didn't you finish? Huh? You think he was happy with me because you have too many clients? No, not Cohen Cage. Just like his daddy. Wants to lock you up in the bedroom and never let you go. I bet you have another little Cage in that belly before too long."

Her face reddens. "I was talking about lunch, you perv! We didn't finish lunch!"

"Hmmm," he mumbles and starts running his hands through my hair. "And what, honey child, was he eating?"

My jaw drops when hers snaps shut and I watch, fascinated, when she turns her eyes to me and with a shrug says, "Sorry. Looks like you're his now." Then stomps off to the back room.

"Uh," I start.

"You need to ignore her, sweetheart. I figured out she was pregnant two weeks ago, mind you she has not a clue, but she will. She always gets snappy in the beginning. So, while I love that I get to get my hands on all this hair, I also get her off her feet while she's back in the breakroom having a snit. So I win, but she wins bigger," he whispers close to my ear and then pulls back.

"Pregnant? Again?"

"I swear it must be a Cage thing. Runs in the family. Super swimmers, both of them."

"Uh," I mumble.

"She'll find out soon enough. If her losing her breakfast this morning was any help, if not, she will when she stops focusing on her best friend's love life long enough to remember she hasn't had her lady time yet."

"Oh my God," I say, still low and soft. Shocked.

"You, sweet girl, are ready for the new you?"

I nod, still thinking about how Sway could know that Dani is pregnant before she does.

"Then sit back and relax, time for me to work my magic."

I nod again, because really what can you do when a man who does heels, skinny jeans and a loose blouse better than you ever could, starts waving his hands around with scissors attached? You sit back and shut the hell up. That's what you do.

"You've had a hard life, honey," he tells me some time later, while painting some high or low or whatever he called them lights. I have no idea; he just said it was time to make my blonde hair come to life.

He looks up from my head and gives me soft, kind eyes. "It takes an old wounded soul to recognize another."

"You?" I don't finish because his eyes get even softer and he nods.

"It isn't easy growing up in the south as a gay man that loves women's clothing. I wouldn't say I'm a cross dresser, but I love what I love and that happens to be heels and tight clothes. It wasn't popular then and it still isn't now. I'm a lucky man though. I have a wonderful husband and a daughter that is my whole entire world. But, all my life until I moved to Hope Town, I felt the pain of my life choices. People think I'm crazy and that's okay with me. I can laugh about it now, but I surround myself with things that make me happy and far as I can see, you're starting to do the same."

"The glitter," I laugh, looking around his station at everything that shines in the lights around the salon.

"Oh yes. Started at church camp. My parents sent me there in hope that I could be saved from the devil that lives inside of me. That, well that backfired when I found art inside that camp. Sitting there during arts and crafts time while the glitter fell through my fingers, I was able to find a little happiness that, as you can see, I keep with me at all times."

I chuckle to myself. He isn't kidding. He really does keep it with him at all times.

"My light in the darkness. We all have that light, honey. Some people, it's an object like glitter. Other people, it's a person that takes their hand and takes the lead."

I look into his eyes. "Is there anything you don't see?" I ask.

"Not often. Plus, I cut Lee's hair the last four times that fine man came in because pregnant patty was too busy taking 'lunch breaks' with her husband."

My laughter comes quick and when Sway starts to freak out because I won't stop moving my head, my laughter climbs. Soon enough, he's joined in and we don't stop joking and laughing until he flips off his blow dryer and turns my chair.

"He isn't going to know what hit him, honey child!" Sway says as my eyes take in the 'new' Megan.

My blonde hair is still blonde, but now there are strips of dark and light blonde, all looks so natural that you would never guess I just spent the last two hours in Sway's hands. I never would have thought that my natural light blonde was a bad look, but now seeing this, I feel like I've been brought to life. My eyes look brighter and my skin looks darker against the softer color.

"You deserve to keep the happiness close to you," he tells me.

"I'm trying," I reply. "Still scares me to pieces."

Which is true. Giving myself to someone, giving them the power over not just my heart, but my daughter's as well and all of it being so new, is scary. It isn't that I don't trust Lee, but when you have had a lot of nothing, then a lot of loss, believing that you can have something beautiful takes time.

"I imagine it does. I'll admit, knowing what you've lost and honey I am sorry for your loss, but knowing that you lost your husband overseas, I was a little shocked you ended up with another man with a dangerous job. You're going to be just—what? What did I say?"

"What's wrong with Megan?" Stella asks and I turn my shocked eyes from Sway to hers and then I look at myself.

Pale skin, wide eyes, and a look of fear.

"What the hell?" My eyes snap to Dani.

"I never even thought about his job," I mumble, my fear taking hold and the roots digging in. "Never once crossed my mind that he . . . good God, he wears a gun . . . and a vest! How could I never even realize how dangerous his job is? Oh my God!"

"Oh, shit," Stella mumbles.

"Oh, no," Sway sighs.

"You, come with me," Dani says softly and pulls me from the

chair. "You stay," she tells Sway. "Let's go." Her hand grabs mine and she starts to walk me toward the room she stomped toward earlier.

I don't resist, too shocked and too busy thinking about all the things that could happen to Lee while on duty to even process anything else.

Dani pushes me down to the couch when we walk into the break room and kneels down in front of me. My panicked eyes not focusing on a thing until she taps me on the cheek. Lightly, but with enough force that the shock of it has my eyes focusing on hers.

"I didn't like that. You made me slap you and that's not something I like. But I really don't like watching you fall back to where you were a year ago. Let me tell you something, honey. Sure, Lee has a job that deals with dangerous situations, but he's a smart man and he's trained. He carries a gun and wears a vest because there may come a time when that's needed, but you cannot let that ruin what you two are starting."

I don't speak.

"Megan. You can't give up on him because his job is a little dangerous. It is nothing like Jack. Nothing. Jack was in a war-torn country and you know without me having to detail it that the types of danger over there are nothing that Lee will have to face."

"I could lose him," I tell her.

"You won't," she states strongly. "You need to talk to him about this."

I nod my head, but know I most likely will not.

"Promise?"

I nod, but don't give her the words. If I don't give her the words then I can keep this to myself until I figure out what to do with it.

Chapter 23

Liam

"YOU OKAY?" I ASK MEGAN for the tenth time tonight.

She looks up from where she had been watching Molly color on her children's menu and gives me a weak smile. Not answering verbally, but telling me without a doubt that she is far from okay with just one look.

I glance at Molly, seated in between us at the half circle table before turning back to Megan. "We're going to talk, darlin'."

Her eyes close and she nods, but again no words.

"Leelee! Look, I made you!"

I continue to look at Megan and try not to let the worry that she's holding something back show on my face when I look at Molly.

Molly turns her menu and when I see what she's drawn, I pull her close and give her a hug.

"Tell me about it?" I ask her.

"Okay! That right there is you," she says pointing to the blue stick figure. "This is Mommy," she continues, pointing to the red one. "This is me," her finger goes to the yellow one. "And this is going to be my baby brother or sister," she finishes, pointing to the little green dot that I didn't even notice before.

I fight to keep my body loose and look over at Megan. Her eyes are wet, but she's holding it back.

"Oh yeah?" I ask Molly, not moving my eyes from Megan.

"Oh yeah," she says in wonderment her melodious voice sparkling with awe. "Can I have a baby now?" Her eyes don't leave mine and I have to work even harder now to push down the emotion that threatens my own chest.

"Little bird," Megan whispers.

"I really want a baby now," Molly returns her own voice now as hushed as her mother's.

"That's not how it works, sweets," Megan continues.

"But, why?"

I clear my throat and move my eyes from Megan's pleading ones to Molly's hopeful ones.

"But you said Leelee is going to stick like gum. You said it. That means if he's my new daddy, that you and Leelee can give me a baby!"

"Hey," I butt in when I see how much this is costing Megan. "I'm already stuck like bubblegum, little lady. Stuck so sticky and gooey that I'll happily be stuck forever. One day, but not now, okay? And Molly, I love you and your mommy, and if one day I'm lucky enough for you to call me daddy, it will stick some more happiness right to my heart with a huge big piece of bubblegum, but I won't be your new daddy. I'll be your other daddy."

"Why?" she asks, her voice still small but her smile big.

"Because you, little lady, already have a daddy and even though he's not here anymore doesn't mean he isn't always with you."

I look up when I hear Megan sniffle and reach out to grab her hand over the table. Molly lets the subject drop, but even through her continuous chatter throughout dinner, Megan remains quiet and I know whatever was weighing on her mind hasn't been made any easier.

"Talk to me, Megan," I demand.

She walks around the couch and sits. I notice, but don't call her out on it, that she purposely placed her body out of arm's length.

Ever since Molly's bomb dropped at dinner, the dark mood she's carried with her since I arrived at the house has continued. I've waited, not wanting to press while Molly was awake, and put on a smile for her sake. But now, Molly is in bed and I'm not putting up with this shit.

"I won't ask again, darlin'. I haven't seen you in over a week, a long week with your goodnight calls being the only thing pushing me through, but now that I finally have you where I want you, you're a million miles away. What gives?"

"Dani's pregnant," she says.

"Good for Dani. Good for Cohen. Not that I'm shocked seeing as they can't keep their hands off each other. Now I know that isn't what has you walking around with the weight of the world on your shoulders, so what. Is. The. Problem?" I push, my frustration clear as can be in my voice.

"You wear a gun," she oddly says.

"Not when I'm off duty. I don't have one on me right now."

"You wear a gun," she repeats, her voice growing louder. Panicked.

"Yeah, Megan. I wear a gun. I'm a cop. We wear guns."

"You wear a vest."

"Yeah. Again, I'm a cop."

"You wear a gun and a vest, Lee!" she shrieks and I draw back at her tone.

"Darlin'," I call, my frustration bleeding out the instant I realized what this is about. "They're to keep me safe."

"You . . . you wear a gun and a vest, Lee," She quivers and wraps her arms around her body.

I don't respond, but I do move so that I can pull her into my arms.

"I thought we were past this, baby. I wear them because for one it's part of my uniform, but they're also there to keep me safe. I know how to work a gun, Megan. I've known how to work one since I was five. I also know what to do if something happens and I need my gun. I'm not going anywhere."

Her body shakes in my hold and her tears wet my shirt.

"Megan, please, darlin', hold onto me and don't let this pull you under."

"Just the thought of something happening to you kills me, Lee. What if something happens for real? What if I lose you too?" she mumbles against my chest after her cries die.

It tears me to my core to see her hurting. I've wondered if something like this would come up, but I never considered her fearing my career. Putting myself in her shoes though, it makes sense, and I kick myself for not seeing it sooner. Preparing for it.

"I'm not going anywhere, Megan. Stuck like gum, remember?"

Her body curls closer and she doesn't speak.

"I love you, Megan. Do you really think, for one second, that now that I have you I wouldn't take every care in the world to make sure I never lose you? That includes my own safety. Things happen, every day things happen, and God willing I hope they never happen to us. If I was ever in the need of my gun or my vest, you have no fears in the knowledge that I will use both to make sure I always come back to you."

Her head comes up and her tear filled eyes blink a few times before she whispers, "You love me?"

"Head over heels, in fucking love, darlin'," I utter back.

"You're in love with me?"

"I'll say it as many times as you need it, but it won't change. I'm in love with you. I love you. I love *you,* Megan—you and Molly. So fucking in love with you that I knew it even before you said your first word to me."

Her tears pick up, this time silent, and her eyes continue to search mine.

"I didn't even pause when your daughter asked me if I was going to be her daddy, not when she asked for a baby, and not when I made it clear to her that should I get that honor—and it would be an honor, Megan—that I would love every second of it. Because I can tell you right now, what we've been building, that's the plan. You, Molly and whatever children you give me will never, for a second, doubt how much I love them."

"Your job is scary dangerous to me, Lee."

"I understand, darlin'. I'm not saying that fear is going to go away, but we will work to make sure you can and know how to handle it, okay?"

She nods her head, the motion making some of the wetness in her eyes roll over and down her cheek.

"You love me?" she probes.

"Fuck, you're cute."

"I love you, Lee. I'm so in love with you that it's terrifying, but what's the most scary is I've never felt like this before. I don't know if I'm doing it right."

My chest swells, my heart speeds up and I swear with the way I feel right now, I might as well be Superman. Fuck, hearing her say that. Knowing that it's costing her to admit, not only to herself but out loud, that she feels love for me that she never felt for her husband.

"There isn't a wrong way to love someone, Megan. You keep giving me you and I swear that you will never regret giving me that."

"I'm still scared, Lee."

"We'll work on that too, darlin'. One step at a time."

She nods.

I close the distance between our mouths and kiss her deep. Deep and full of unspoken promise. "Go check to make sure Molly is sleeping, baby."

She doesn't move. Her eyes still half mast and if I had to guess, she hasn't come out of the fog that kiss put over her.

"Megan. Go make sure Molly is sleeping. And do it quick before I strip you down and fuck you right here."

She almost trips over her feet when she hurries off the couch and back down the hall. I take my time, making sure the door is locked and the house is shut down, because I have no intention of leaving after tonight.

Chapter 24

Liam

"SHE'S ASLEEP. OUT COLD," SHE tells me and steps toward where I've been waiting. I moved to the hallway outside of Molly's room after turning all the lights off in the house and checking the lock on both front and back doors.

"I know we said we wouldn't do this until Molly had time to adjust, but baby she asked us for a baby tonight, I'm pretty sure that's as adjusted as it gets. I need to get you naked and my mouth on you so I can remind you why you love me so much."

I started stalking toward her before I finished speaking and without waiting for her to speak, I pull her into my arms and drop my mouth to hers. My body pushes hers into the wall next to her bedroom door and my hands grab her hips to pull her closer.

"I'm not leaving, Megan."

One hand goes up and I take her full breast in my hand, giving her a squeeze and then thumbing her nipple. Her head falls back against the wall and she moans.

"I don't want you to leave, Lee," she pants against my mouth.

"I'm not talking about tonight, Megan, even though I'm not leaving tonight either. I mean, I'm not going anywhere, darlin'."

She pushes up on her toes and I bend, helping her get my mouth. Letting her take the lead, I open my mouth when her tongue presses against my lips. The second my mouth opens, the kiss turns hungry and her hands claw at my arms. I bend and place her ass in my hands. She doesn't hesitate to give a little jump and as I lift, her legs wrap around my waist. She deepens the kiss and as our tongues swirl together she starts rocking her pussy against my hard cock. She's got on another pair of short shorts and through the thin material I can feel the heat of her, making me groan, and then rock my hips forward when she answers me with one of her own.

I fumble slightly, but make my way into her bedroom without breaking our connection once. Turning before I sit on her bed, I move us until my back is against her wooden headboard and her legs are wide on either side of my hips.

"I don't have any condoms here," she blurts after pulling her lips from mine.

I take a deep breath and give her a reassuring smile.

"Are you clean?" I ask, knowing her answer.

"Of course, yes."

"I'm checked, often, for work. But even if I wasn't, I haven't had anyone but you in over a year. It's your call, but darlin', I would love to feel you with nothing between us."

"I'm on the pill. Regulates me, I mean . . . we're good."

"Then no more condoms, baby," I tell her with a grin and move my lips back to hers as she blushes.

My hands move from her ass, under her shirt and up her sides. When I hit her bra, it takes one flip of my wrist to open the clasps. She pushes herself from my mouth with a gasp, moves back so my hands fall to the sides and while looking me in the eye, pulls both her shirt and bra off. Not a second later, her mouth is back on mine and her small hands are pulling at my shirt.

"Darlin', what's the hurry?" I ask when I pull back to remove the shirt that she has been so desperately trying to claw to shreds.

Her breathing is coming rapidly and she lets her head roll back as her hips continue to rock against mine. I'm not even sure she heard me.

"I need to feel you." Her voice is wild, anxious, and I know in that moment that this is something more than sex.

More than making love.

More than just *us.*

It hits me, that after everything that's been running through her head today, that she really does need this. She needs to feel me and know that I'm still here.

"Then take me, darlin'," I tell her and look deep in her eyes, hoping that with that look I'm showing her how much I love her. "Take me. Take everything, Megan."

She makes a noise. It's a heartbreaking mix between a cry and a moan before her hands come forward and she starts to desperately claw at my belt, needing it out of the way with a fever that has her crying out when it doesn't unhook right away. I give her what she needs; helping her undo my belt and I push her hands aside when she goes to my jeans, knowing that she will just get frustrated again.

She scurries off my lap and I watch, while pulling the buttons on my jeans apart, as the rest of her clothes come off. Before I can push my jeans any further than down my hips and around my ass, she's back in my lap, her lips on mine the second that her ass hits my lap. This time, I help build the kiss and pray that some of that desperation will be healed when she takes me.

Her small hands come up and she takes my face between them, slowing her kiss down until her tongue is making lazy sweeps.

"Darlin'," I moan when she starts to rock against me. "What do you need?"

"You. Just you," she answers.

"Then. Take. Me."

She doesn't. She looks into my eyes, hers still holding onto her fear, but she does not take me.

"Megan. I'm here. Fuck, baby, I'm close to coming with just feeling your wet pussy against my cock. Please, take me."

Again, she doesn't move.

"Megan."

Nothing.

"Darlin'," I murmur, my hands coming up to curl around her neck.

At my touch, her eyes drop and my heart clenches when I see a tear roll out.

"Baby," Kiss. "Please, take me."

She opens her eyes and shakes her head.

"Megan," I start, my own worry starting to climb, causing me to hold my breath when she interrupts me.

"Help me," she whimpers.

I give her a squeeze with my hands resting on her hips and cock my brow, letting her know without words that she never has to doubt. She pushes up with her thighs as I help lift her weight and one hand comes off my shoulders to wrap around my cock. I moan the second her fingers close around me and my hips jerk. Fuck me, it's going to take an act of God to last longer than a second.

With her eyes locked on mine, she drops down until her ass is flush to my thighs and my cock is deep inside her wet pussy. She doesn't move past the slow rocking of her hips.

"Megan, take me. Take what you need to know I'm right here," I beg and relax the bruising hold my fingers have on her hips.

It's fascinating to watch, the way that she is healing with just a connection to my body, but as she slowly rocks, the fear that had been prominent in her gaze weakens until it's all but gone. In its place, hope and love start to burn bright. The worry lines around her eyes, fade, and the tight pinch of her lips relaxes until her mouth is parted with gasping pants. Finally, the tiny furrow of her brows pulls back and when her eyes fill with tears this time I know they aren't anywhere close to the ones that wept out earlier.

These are tears that recognize what we're doing.

Feeling tears.

Tears that don't just feel a little—they feel everything.

Her hands roam over my chest, until she pushes them up to curl around my shoulders. Mine move from her hips and up her torso until both of her full breasts are in my hands. I roll her nipples between my fingers. Her breathing hitches and I release her nipples and run my fingertips down her body, lightly grazing. My eyes follow the path as goosebumps spark all over her body, followed by a quiver that lightly jolts her body.

When my hands move back to her hips, I give her a squeeze. "Take it."

Her eyes close at my demand. And then, she takes it.

The hands at my shoulders dig deep, until I know I'll have her nails indenting the skin when we finish, and those thighs start moving. Up slowly, just to slam her body down before rocking forward. She repeats her movements, each time building in speed. It takes every ounce of willpower to keep my body still and let her take what she needs when all I want to do is flip her to her back and pound into her. My cock is aching from the force of my desire.

"Take it, Megan. Fuck me, take it, darlin'."

She moans and speeds up again, this time her movements jerky and I know she's close.

"God, you feel so fucking good taking my cock."

"Lee," she moans.

"Take it."

Her head moves and those nails dig deeper. Then her lips are on mine and with her tongue dancing with mine, I swallow her screams.

I pull back when I feel the last spasm against my cock and look into her heavy eyes. "You need me to take over baby? Rock hard and the way you're coating my balls with your come is only making me harder."

She hums and nods her head before taking my mouth again. When I flip her to her back, her head is hanging off the bottom of her bed. Thankfully she has a bed with just a headboard, giving me more room to play. I lift up on my knees until I'm kneeling with her pussy still clamped tight around me then I lift her hips a little more until just her shoulders are resting against the bed.

"You need something to hold on to?"

I feel her walls give a squeeze and her head rolls.

Pushing in while I lift off from kneeling has my cock hitting her deeper than I have before. Her hands come up from fisting the sheets next to us and wrap around my wrists. When I sink back in, rocking her body with the force of my thrust, her head comes up and her eyes shoot to where my cock is gliding in and out of her body. Wet with her juices.

We both moan.

"Please," she begs.

Sweat drops down my back and I lean forward, panting. I lose the hold I had on her hips and move my hands to the bed, hovering just above her while my cock is still deep.

"Please what, darlin'. Tell me what you need."

"I need to feel all of you," she says softly. "Cover me and take me, but I have to feel you."

Understanding hits and my heart pounds even quicker. God, my sweet girl. She might understand that while my job holds a fraction of the danger that her husband's did, but she needs to rid herself of those ghosts today's spell brought back, by reminding herself that I am very much alive.

And to do that, she needs to feel.

Feel alive.

I close my eyes and drop my head to hers. My body follows until I've given her as much weight as I can. Her legs come up and wrap tightly around my hips. I feel her arms at my side and then around my back. Then, her head comes up and her mouth fuses with mine.

Only then, when she's completely wrapped herself around me, do I continue to move inside her. My arms against the mattress, elbows digging in, and hands in her hair. There isn't an inch of our bodies that doesn't feel the other. Even though my body is screaming for it, I rock slowly, and give her everything that she needs.

With each thrust, I pray that she feels what she needs. Our lips never part and when I feel her walls tighten and her wetness coat my cock, only then do I push deep and come harder than I've ever felt before.

"I love you," she whispers in my ear, her breathing coming in choked pants.

"I love you, too, Megan. So much, darlin'."

Chapter 25

Megan

*I*T'S BEEN A MONTH SINCE I lost my mind over Lee's job. A month of him handling me with care, but also a month that's been full of healing. It's been hard at times, but he's been there for every stumble to help pick me back up. At his urging I started seeing a grief counselor. I'll admit now that it's a step I should have taken on my own years ago, but with both of their help, I've been able to let go of almost all of my pain. Lee started coming to my twice a week meetings at the counselor's urging. It started about three weeks after I started going and I'm glad I made that step. Having him with me, his hand in mine, was a strength I needed to get through some hard memories.

It was also through those meetings that he made it clear, sometimes with and sometimes without words that a huge part of him fell in love with me because of my strength. I didn't understand it, because I've felt nothing but weakness, but Lee told me, in those meetings, that only a person with a strength of an army would keep fighting to live. I couldn't see it, living in pain, but he's right—something I can see now—I've been fighting my whole life. Losing Jack was a hard blow and even though it took me a long time to battle the depression his death set upon me, I never gave up.

Another milestone that we made as our new threesome, was Lee's relationship with Molly. I haven't been shocked that she fell into her love for him easily, that's just who Molly is. She doesn't doubt her feelings.

Needless to say, they have been inseparable. Regardless of if we're at our house, his, or out, my daughter is always as close as she can get to him. Lee and I talked about it and we both agree that it is just the way Molly is. She wants him to know how much he means to her, but because she's so young she doesn't know how to verbalize it, instead she gives him what she can. Herself.

Seeing them together was a big part in my healing. Seeing that she loves him as much as I do, gives me the reassurance that we're where we're meant to be.

Lee showed me again how big his heart was when he fell into his new role as a father figure with effortless ease. His protective nature only adding to the power in which his bond formed with her. You can tell, there is nothing but love that he feels for his girls.

And that's what we've become—gladly—to him. We're his girls and he . . . he is our man.

Today is my last step in letting go. One that I've been putting off, but now I know needs to happen for us all to move on completely pain free. I don't think I was putting it off because I wasn't ready, but more that I didn't know how to do it or what to say.

How do you tell your dead husband that you've moved on?

I look up and see Lee walking with Molly as I trail behind them. When we got to the graveyard he had asked for me to give him a second and then took off in the direction I had told him when he asked where Jack was. When he reached his hand out for Molly's my reaction couldn't be stopped. I gasped, but Lee being his confident self, just gave me soft eyes.

Which leads me to now, as I watch them strolling through the headstones hand in hand. I move to a bench about ten paces from Jack's spot and wait. I used to only come every month, sometimes when the pain was too much, I wouldn't come until it eased up a little. Now, for the last year, I've been coming with Molly every two weeks. This, however, is the first time we've asked Lee to come.

Lee stops and I see him reading over the headstone, then he kneels and pulls Molly closer. Her little arms hug his back and her head turns to rest against his shoulder.

When his lips start moving, facing Jack, my heart speeds up and deep down I know he isn't talking to Molly. She doesn't move, but her arm pulls his shirt as her fist grabs hold of the material.

Call it an invasion of his privacy, whatever you want, but nothing in that moment could have kept me from walking over. My eyes don't leave where they're at, his head turns but his words don't stop and he turns back, acknowledging that I'm coming regardless, but he doesn't stop.

Then his words hit my ears.

And if I had any fears left in my body about this new path for Molly and me, they vanished in a heartbeat.

"Like I said, you don't know me, but I like to think we would have gotten along. Hell, we might have played golf on my off days, had beers while watching the game, who knows. I hate thinking it, because it isn't fair that you lost your way, but when you did, it made it possible for me to find mine. It gave me my girls and I wouldn't be the man I am right now without their love. Rest easy knowing that not a day will pass that I won't make sure they know how grateful I am that I've been given that gift. Not a day will pass that I don't show them how much I love them in return. I'll fight to keep them safe. I would give my own life to make that promise a reality if need be. And one day, if Molly decides it so, I hope to share the title you had while in her world, but if that day never comes, I'll still love her as if she was my own. I owe you my thanks and so much more for loving Megan and bringing her everything she needed while you were here. You have no worries now, brother, knowing that I'll do everything in my power to give them the world. They've both given me everything I've dreamt of just by handing over their love and I'll never take that for granted."

My God.

This man.

I move forward and take the last two steps that take me to his side. My hand comes out and I run my fingers through his hair.

"Hey, Jack," I say and continue my sweep of his thick hair. "I guess you met Lee."

I hear both Lee and Molly laugh, but I keep my eyes pinned to the stone in front of me.

"I miss you, Jack." I tell the stone. "I miss you, but that's okay. It doesn't hurt anymore." Lee's hand moves and I feel him reach out to grab the hand that isn't playing with his hair. I can't stop my movements. Touching Lee, having that, is keeping me grounded right now. "Molly is so big. The top of her head hits Lee right at his belt. She does this really cute thing when she sees him in uniform—he's a cop, you know—and thinks it's hilarious that she can't give him a hug with his belt on because all of his special police stuff whomps her in the head." I take a deep breath, calming my racing heart and hopefully stopping my rambling. "Anyway. I'm happy, Jack. So happy that sometimes I think my heart is going to burst right out of my body. I get these waves in my stomach when Lee's around and sometimes I feel like I might puke," I stop when I feel Lee's body moving as he laughs. "What?"

"Darlin', not sure it's a good thing I make you want to puke," he laughs.

"Mommy that's icky," Molly chimes in.

I roll my eyes at the stone and continue. "Anyway. I feel, Jack, I feel so much and for a long while I didn't feel anything. You left and I just felt emptiness and pain. Now it's like I feel everything, but those feelings are amplified. It's so beautiful."

The headstone doesn't reply. The breeze around us picks up and I smile into the wind.

"I love you, Jack. You gave me and Molly a beautiful life and even though you had to leave us, that beautiful life turned into a beautiful forever."

Lee's hand gives me another squeeze and I lose my hold on his hair when he stands, taking Molly up with him. His arm goes around my shoulders and when I'm pulled into his side, I wrap my arms around him. In the end, both Molly and I have Lee in the circle of our arms as he holds us tight.

"You gave me the world, Jack. I can never thank you enough for that kind of gift. Rest easy."

Molly looks away from Lee when he finishes and whispers toward the stone, "I love you, Daddy."

And with dry eyes watching the wind quiet, I tell my husband goodbye. "We love you, forever, Jack. We'll miss you just as long. I know somewhere up there you're smiling huge and loving the fact that I'm living a life that's full and I promise you that I will take each day head on looking forward to that beauty."

When we turn to walk back to Lee's truck, not once do any one of us let our hold slip.

Chapter 26

Megan

"DON'T BE NERVOUS," LEE TELLS me, tightening his hold on my clammy hand.

"What's that mean?" Molly asks from her perch in Lee's other arm.

"Your mommy has so many butterflies in her belly she's about to squeeze off my fingers, her hand's holding mine so tight. So many little ticklish butterflies in her belly," Lee's deep voice rumbles in response.

"Why did you put butterflies in there, Mommy?" her melodious voice chirps, easing some of my nerves.

I turn my head, looking away from the front door of Lee's family home, and before looking at my beautiful daughter; I stare at the strong man holding her. His warm gaze bringing a deep breath to my lungs that washes over me like a calming touch.

"Lee," my voice sounds in hushed tones.

"I asked you a while ago to just take my hand, darlin', I wasn't just asking you to do the action. It was my nonverbal promise to you that I wouldn't let go. Each step forward, we do together. I'm here and I'm not letting go. You've got not one thing to be nervous about, but I understand why you are. They're going to love you and they're going to love Molly. Not just because I love you both, but also because if anyone knows what it feels like to overcome from pain to find beauty, it's my parents. Trust me, okay?"

His hand gives me a squeeze and even though I still feel some of those nerves, he's right. I've never been given a reason to question that.

"She's got princess shoes," Molly whispers in Lee's ear loud enough that I move my eyes from his, up to hers and then follow them forward to see his mom standing in the doorway, wringing her own hands in front of her nervously.

Of course I know who his parents are. In the last two years of me being pulled into the fold, I've been to a few gatherings where all the parents were also in attendance. I also know that she's Dani's mom's best friend and has been for years and years before they had Dani and Lee, thus the reason that Dani and Lee were destined to be best friends even before birth.

But besides the small smile in passing, I've never spoken to either of them.

Add to that the small fact that their son has fallen in love with a woman with baggage of a widowed mom.

A woman, that until about five months ago, hasn't been able to see the beauty in life past her guilt filled grief.

A woman that they very well may see as someone not good enough for their son.

And that's what's been keeping me so full of nerves that I've been on the edge of puking all day.

"She always has princess shoes on, little lady. Even when she's cleaning the house or doing laundry. My mom, she's a silly girl."

Lee's voice pulls me back from my scared thoughts and I steady my breathing, give him a squeeze and when his feet start carrying us up the driveway, toward his waiting mother, I follow and pray that I don't make a fool of myself.

And that his mother won't see Molly and me as the wrong choice for her son's future.

"Hey, Mom," he greets when we reach the front porch. "Meet my girls, Molly and Megan."

I gulp and give her what I hope is a welcoming smile. She looks at her son with love in her eyes before they turn to me.

"Megan," she breathes. "It's so good to finally, formally, meet you. We've been waiting for this."

"Uh, hi," I squeak and Molly laughs.

"Mommy has butterflies all inside her belly. Leelee told me so."

I feel my face heat and my hand gets a gentle tug. I look up and meet Lee's gaze. He gives me a wink and then his face washes with love and compassion. His expression filling my heart instantly with his love and effectively kicking the crap out of those butterflies.

Turning back to his mom, I reach out my hand, and blurt, "I

did. They were crazy butterflies that fluttered their wings so much I couldn't take a deep breath. So, hi, I'm Megan and I'm absolutely terrified that you won't like me."

I feel Lee shaking with his amusement, but my eyes are transfixed on his mom as I watch, with fascination, as her eyes, so much like Lee's, fill with understanding before my hand is knocked to the side as her body moves forward. Her arms reach out and wrap around my middle and then she gives me a hug that knocks the wind out of my chest with her strength.

"Oh, honey. I was in love with you before I even knew who had stolen my son's heart. Have no worries about that. You keep doing whatever has that smile on my boy's face. I swear, it's been like watching his father all over again these last few months."

I don't know what to say. Or do. So I follow my gut, drop Lee's hand, and hug his mom back just as tight.

"He's easy to love," I tell her honestly.

"I know," she whispers. "It's a Beckett thing."

I laugh, but don't let go.

"Uh, Mom. You think I could have my woman back now?" Lee laughs.

"No, you can't," she snaps and continues to hug me tight.

"Dee, baby, let go of Lee's woman and let them come inside."

I open my eyes at the new voice and look up into Lee's father's eyes. If I thought he looked like his mom, I was wrong. Lee is the spitting image of his father and I have no doubt that when Lee gets older, his good looks will only become richer. John Beckett, or Beck as I've heard so many call him, has the same thick dark brown hair as his son. His strong bone structure a mirror to his son's. You can tell that he laughs hard, and often, because the smile lines on his tan face are deep, even when he's just smirking.

Lee's dad is smoking hot.

Of course, his mom is downright stunning too, so it isn't a shock to me that Lee is as handsome as he is.

"You look like my Leelee," Molly states in awe.

"Hey, sweet girl, I sure do. Want to know why?" Lee's dad asks her.

"Yup!" she shouts.

Lee's dad chuckles deep in his throat, "That's because he's my Lee too. We're his mom and dad. He looks like us just like you look like your mom."

When Dee lets go of my body, I turn and watch Molly move her eyes from Lee's smiling face, back to his father's. Then in typical Molly fashion, she gives out more of her love.

"Yay! That means you're mine too. I get to keep you and I'm never, ever, ever going to give you away! Do you want a make-upover?" she exclaims in rushed excitement. "Mommy, yay!" she finishes at a whisper. "We get more."

And just like that, a sense of calm I never thought possible earlier today rushes over me and I smile at my daughter. "We sure do, little bird. So much so, that we have everything."

Lee reaches out and grabs my hand, this time not to give re-assurance in the face of my nerves, but to confirm that we do, in fact, have everything.

"Right," Lee's mom speaks, but pauses to clear her throat. When I look back to her, her eyes are misty and she gives me a smile. "Well, now that that's settled. Molly, do you want to come and help me make the table?"

Molly gives Lee a hug around his neck, kisses his check, and then asks, "Can I go play with your mommy, Leelee?"

"Call me, Dee, baby. I have a feeling that will change soon though," she oddly adds, making her husband laugh low in his throat

"Leelee, can I go play with mommy Dee?"

God, my girl.

Lee gives her a nod and with a smile, sets her on her feet. She doesn't waste a second taking Dee's offered hand and following her into the house.

"Nice to finally meet you, Megan. You've made our boy real happy," his dad says when Molly and his wife move out of sight.

Turning back to him, I take his offered hand. "It's a pleasure to meet you, Mr. Beckett," I respond and stiffen when he starts to laugh. The lines around his eyes deepening with his mirth.

"Call me Beck, honey, everyone does."

"All right, Mr. Beck," I confirm.

He laughs harder. This time Lee annoyingly joins in.

"Just Beck, drop the mister. We're family here and Megan . . . welcome to the family."

Family. I nod, not trusting my voice. Just like that his parents have openly accepted both Molly and me, giving us the family I always wanted for my daughter. One that loves without reservations and opens their arms immediately, no questions asked, to give that love freely.

When Jack and I were married, we knew that we would never be able to give Molly this. My parents, being the drunken, drug filled messes they were, have been long since forgotten. Jack's parents were just as bad. His mom died when he was younger and his dad; never able to put the bottle down before that, never fell into his role as a parent. Thus, Jack was just Jack. We learned his father had passed away a few months after we married and left town. Knowing all that, we were okay that Molly would have only us. It wasn't until recently that I realized how much it had bothered me that she wouldn't have a large family full of love.

I look up at Lee and smile, brightly, thankful for yet another gift this man made a reality, when his unwavering determination to make us an "us" has paid off. It was through his strength and love that we have a future so bright it burns.

This time, that burn, one I had felt differently before, was welcome. Before I had no ashes left to be reborn from, because the pain burned too strong. But now, because of the burn of his love on our life, taking away the ashes left from my guilt and suffering, I just know the new life born from the last will be overrun with love and happiness.

It's our future.

"And this one, well, our Liam went through a stage that lasted almost six months. In that time he was naked every time we turned around. Beck thought this was hilarious, which is why there are so many pictures. I, however, did not. Do you know how embarrassing it is when your son gets buck naked in the middle of the supermarket?"

I shake my head and laugh even harder than I had in the last hour of Dee showing me old pictures of Lee. Once I got over my nerves, it was like I had been a part of this family forever. Molly has been on cloud nine too. Going from helping his mom set out the takeout—because according to Dee, she does not cook—then talking Beck's ear off about all the things we do as a threesome, to which Beck's handsome smile grew even larger, and those lines got even deeper.

"But I got him back, his father I mean. He didn't think it was funny when our little nudist stopped being a nudist and started wearing my heels all over the house. Oh, he didn't think that was funny one bit, but I did. God didn't see it fit for us to have a girl, but he did give me a boy that had no problems walking in four-inch heels," she laughs.

"He didn't," I gasp, shocked at the picture before me of Lee. He looks to be Molly's age, huge smile, dimple sticking out and his mother's bright red heels on his feet. "Oh my God, he did!" My giggles turn into deep belly laughs at this point.

"What are you two in here cackling about?" Beck asks, rounding the couch and settling in next to his wife. "Oh Dee, your son is going to kill you," he gruffs with a smile.

"Oh hush, old man. He isn't going to do anything of the sort."

"If you don't stop showing his woman all those embarrassing pictures of him, he will."

She turns and narrows her eyes at her husband. "I've been waiting his whole life for this moment. When my little man would bring home his future. All my life, John Beckett. You do not spoil this for me."

I wouldn't have guessed, because she seems so soft-spoken and sweet, that his mom would have a backbone that would snap tight, but I was wrong. She may look the part of quiet and motherly, but right in this moment, I can tell where Lee got a lot of his stubborn grit.

Beck's eyes soften and he gazes at his wife with love written all over his body. "Pull those claws back, wildcat," he hums, his voice sounding deeper, rawer, and I instantly feel like I'm intruding on something a little too intimate.

"Would you two stop?" Lee laughs and drops down next to me. His eyes hit the open photo album seconds before shooting back to his mom. "You didn't," he groans.

"I did. Don't you start on me either, Liam. I'm your mother and it's my mother duty to share all of your embarrassing moments with your girlfriend. You haven't given me the chance before and if I'm judging right, I won't need another, so I'm taking it and you can just deal."

Lee puts his hands up, surrendering to his mom, and pulls me back to his chest.

"Molly, come here, little lady! Old grandma Dee has some funny pictures to show you."

Dee's eyes narrow at his reference to her age, but when Molly comes skipping into the room, her face goes soft. "Just Grandma, honey or nanny works too. Don't listen to that grumpy man. He's just mad he doesn't fit in my shoes anymore," Dee tells her and we all laugh when Lee starts to sputter.

We continue looking through the photo albums, laughing when Lee gets embarrassed, but true to her word, his mom doesn't stop until the last book is finished.

"That was a terrible thing to do to your only son," he grumbles and leans back crossing his arms over his chest.

"Mommy, Leelee is having a fit," Molly snickers.

"He sure is, little bird," I tease.

"You just wait, Liam," Dee starts. "You just wait." She looks over at me, "You make sure and take lots of pictures of Molly and any more children you're blessed with. You'll love this moment just as much as I have. I don't have a daughter, but I'm sure if I did, this lump here would be doing the same thing I just did," she says and points to Beck before laughing when he pulls her to his side.

"The hell I would," he rumbles, giving her a soft kiss before looking at me. "But I would be cleaning every gun I own at the approximate time that any man was due to arrive," he tells me in all seriousness.

"That's not a bad idea," Lee mutters to himself and I look over at him. "What?" he questions, throwing his hands up. "It's a good idea. When Molly starts dating it's also one I won't forget."

"What?" I ask lamely.

"Darlin', she looks like your twin now at five. Add ten years to that and I'm going to go out of my mind when boys start coming around."

His parents laugh and Molly joins in, but I just look at him. Right when I'm about to respond he opens his mouth and shocks me again.

"You give me more girls and I'll have to buy more guns though. You give me some boys and I'll make sure they know how to help me clean those guns. I figure though, with me being a cop, there isn't going to be a single knucklehead that messes with my girl."

"What's a knucklehead," Molly questions, breaking into my thoughts.

"Boys are knuckleheads," Lee tells her. "And I don't want knuckleheads near my girl."

His parent's laughter grows.

"That's me, right?" Molly inquires.

"That's right, little lady. You're all mine forever and ever."

She twitters a laugh that sounds like a happier version of her chirpy bird giggles.

"Mommy, I love being Leelee's girl."

I don't hear his parents laughing now. My eyes don't leave Molly's when I nod and tell her how much I love that too. But I don't need to see his parents to know how happy they are for their son.

When Molly's arms reach out and wrap around both mine and Lee's neck, I hug her back and close my eyes, loving every second of our little threesome. But my thoughts are confirmed when I hear his dad, gruff voice that is thick with emotion, tell his son four words that make my throat thick with emotion.

"Proud of you, son."

Chapter 27

Megan

AS PROMISED, LEE'S WORK SCHEDULE and the rain finally synced up. Last night, while watching Lee and Molly have the cutest tea party I've ever seen, it started to rain. Not just any rain, this one shook the whole house with its power. Lee stops, teapot in hand mid pour, looks at me across the room. His smile was no less knee-melting, but it held a youthful excitement to it that had me pausing.

I've seen a lot of Lee smiles in the past. The ones when I first started coming around, before we came together, held mischief. After our first night together, they held promise of his determination. Then, while I was busy ignoring and avoiding, even though his smile still held that determination, there was also a small hint to what my avoidance was doing to him. A little dip on the left side that prevented his dimple from coming all the way out, a little dip that showed me it cost him to keep his distance. Now, the only smile he gives us is one that expresses his love toward Molly and me.

Until this one.

This new one that I've never seen.

And mixed with the love on his face, this exuberance toward something as simple as rain, gives my heart pause before picking back up as if it's in the race of a lifetime.

It's feels freaking amazing.

"It's raining, darlin'," he told me.

"Cats and dogs," Molly jokes.

He looks across the expanse of the tea party covered table. "Yeah, little lady, huge dogs and fat cats. Do you hear how loud they are?"

She giggles, "You're silly, Leelee!"

He puts the teapot down and runs his hand over her ringlets, nodding, before standing from his spot and walks around the coffee table until he's standing just feet in front of me.

"It's raining," he repeats.

I nod.

"And I'm off tomorrow," he oddly states.

I nod again because really, he's telling me something I already know.

"Change of plans. Can you lose a day of writing and it not affect your deadline?"

"Uh, yeah?"

"Can you really? Or are you just telling me what I want to

hear? There isn't a right answer, baby, if you can't take the time, we won't. You told me last week that you were stressed about your deadline with your editor pushing into the time you needed to have it to formatting."

Okay, so to be honest, I can't really give up a day. I've been working on my first self-published title I've released in three years. A title that means the freaking world to me because the plot mirrors mine and Lee's relationship closely. A second chance love story that holds so much of me between those pages that even if I wasn't on deadline panic mode, I would still be in panic mode.

The Healing Hand, with the urging of my grief counselor, was what I needed to take the last pieces of my pain, guilt, and grief into a tangible form that would help me heal. It's been an emotional journey the last eight weeks that I've been working on it, but Lee's been by my side every step of the way. He held me when the scenes became too much that I had to stop. The tears that I shed during those chapters, cathartic in the sense that each warm drop felt like it leaked the pain straight from my soul.

However, seeing Lee so excited over whatever he's plotting, has me saying, "Of course I can take the day off," with no doubt in my mind that it will be worth the extra hours of late night typing.

His face goes soft, but he doesn't lose an ounce of excitement. He sees right through me, but doesn't call me out.

"I'll call Dani, make sure she's off to watch the little lady. If not, I know Izzy is around. But, baby, my mom has been itching for some Molly time."

I give him a smile, "Then, honey, call your mom."

His dimple comes out and I can tell how much that answer

means to him. In the last six weeks since our first dinner at his parent's house, we've had dinner there every Sunday since. Molly has dropped the first names and they are now Nanna and Pops. It's rare that Dani watches her when Lee wants to go on a date night. Now Molly has two grandmother figures, Izzy and Dee that seem to take great joy in fighting over her.

I lose his eyes when he moves his gaze to his phone, but hear him when he so oddly says. "Got it. Get ready for your feel trip." Then his thumb starts moving over his phone and when he looks up, all I get is a wink before his call is connected.

Did he say feel trip? I listen, distractedly, as he talks to his mom. Not that I'm surprised, but she immediately asked for Molly to spend the night, to which Lee agreed after checking with me.

"I'm not sure why you asked my permission, honey," I tell him after he disconnects the call. "What?" I question when he looks at me like I've lost my mind.

"Darlin', nothing would make me happier if Molly was mine, but until the day we make that official, I'm not the one that has the power to make that call."

"Yes you do," I tell him, not understanding completely.

"No, Megan. I do not."

I look over at Molly to make sure she isn't listening and grab his hand, pulling him into the kitchen. "Where is this coming from?"

He sighs, "You know I love you? Both of you?" he asks.

"Of course I do."

"One day, God I hope I'm lucky enough, when I put my ring on your finger and you become my wife, then I hope Molly gives me the blessing of being a man she calls daddy. One day, when we take that step, then yeah I would feel like I have the go to make a call on whether she stays with my mom or Dani. But bottom line, I don't yet and I have enough respect for you to ask."

I close the distance between us and smile up at him. "You have no clue how much that little girl loves you, honey, but I understand. I don't agree with you, but that's because in my eyes, you already hold that right. And one day, if *I'm* lucky enough, I'll enjoy those rings on my finger." I lean up on my toes and give his slack jaw a kiss, loving the way that my lips tickle against his stubble. "I'm going to put *our* girl to sleep, you want to come tuck her in with me?"

He seems to visibly shake himself from the shock that held him still, then with a small smirk on his lips, follows me to get Molly ready for bed.

"Are you sure about this?" I ask Lee.

"Darlin'," he replies but gives me nothing more.

"You're so annoying sometimes."

He laughs and the vibrations tickle my palms, matching the vibrations that are doing nothing to squelch the arousal that having his body pressed close to my front gives me.

"Ready?" He asks, turning his head slightly, giving me his dimple.

"Uh," I sputter and look away from his dimple and across the rain-soaked, mud-filled, expanse of earth in front of us.

"You're ready," he laughs. "Just hold on, Megan. Hold on and feel."

"Again with this?" I retort then snap my mouth shut when he hits the gas.

My fingers dig into his shirt and my thighs tighten around his strong body. I feel the wind whipping against my face, my hair flying behind us as we speed up, and then . . . my stomach comes flying up to my throat and all I feel is cold before my eyes shut tight and wetness coats my skin.

"Holy shit," I breathe.

When I finally feel like my stomach might have returned back to my gut, I open my eyes and watch as the trees blur by us. Lee holds the handles with his usual confidence and I know, even though I'm scared out of my mind, that he won't let anything happen to us.

I lean forward, the helmet he insisted I wear even though he isn't wearing one, tapping his on the side of his head, and do as he instructed. I hold on and feel.

He takes the winding trails for what feels like hours. The roar of his ATV trailing behind us with his speed. He doesn't shy away from those big, mud-filled puddles, nope. Not my Lee. He spots one and it's full fury of his speed powering through them. The first time that the muddy water coated us both, I almost had a heart attack. Mainly because I thought it would be like the first puddle we hit that was full of just rain water, splashing us and then just leaving wet marks behind. No. Not these monster baby lakes filled with muddy water. Okay, slight exaggeration, but that's sure what it felt like.

He moved down from the trail we had just been climbing and started to take the steep dirt path downward. Not paying a bit of attention to the trail because I was too focused on wondering how hard it would be to get myself off using his body and the vibrations, when his nose end hit the mud first, a huge wave of brown wetness covered us. And of course, because I was too busy trying to work at getting myself off, my back was arched. I had, in my mind, the best plan to arch my back and rub my core against the seat and his hard body. But when that mud wave came up and then back down, it shot straight down the back of my pants.

"Oh, my God, Lee!"

He doesn't answer, just laughs harder. So hard, in fact, that he has to stop the four-wheeler.

"This isn't funny! I have mud . . . oh my God . . . I have mud in my ass!"

His laughter picks up until he is forced to hold his sides.

"Holy crap. I can feel it. It's all in my panties, Lee!"

Again, the big jerk just keeps on laughing until he has to pull his shirt up, flip it to the inside and wipe the tears his laughing has caused, rolling down his face.

"I swear, Liam Beckett. I was this close, this freaking close," I scream, holding my pointer finger just an inch from my thumb, "To having one hell of an orgasm. It was building so high, I was too busy wondering if I would fall off the back when I went off. This freaking close and now . . . now I have mud in my ASS!"

Too busy flipping out, I didn't even notice when Lee stopped laughing. That is, until he moved and jumped from the seat. He reached out, grabbed my hips and in a move I still can't process, his ass was back in the seat with me facing him. Our muddy covered chests pressed tight and his mouth on mine in a bruising kiss.

All of the mud is forgotten as his lips plunder mine. My fingers curl into his shoulders and I moan deep into his mouth.

He pulls back and searches my eyes.

"How was that feel trip, Megan?" he says in a growl, the soft look in his eyes betrayed by how forceful he spoke.

"Huh?" I ask in a daze.

"Fuck me," he says hoarsely. "Fucking, fuck me."

"That . . . uh, would be nice, but seeing as I have mud in places mud shouldn't be, I would be worried about infection." I tell him in all seriousness.

"Fuck."

"Yup."

"I didn't want to stop so soon, but I take it by the fact that you laughed so hard before that last puddle that I have no doubt you felt and all that you were feeling was nothing but excitement. You took something you were dead set wouldn't be a bit of fun, braved it, and had fun. That is until I ruined your orgasm, so as far as I can see my job here is done and I should make up for that lost release."

"Uh, baby, I'm not following," I tell him.

"I imagine you aren't. Feel trip over, darlin'. We get back home, I show you my list and then I fuck you hard."

"Your list?"

"Yeah. My list is about to change. My girl feels, freely and happily, with no small amount of brave courage. Time to take that list and turn it into a bucket."

"You make no sense."

He just smiles and nods. When we situate ourselves back on the seat, he takes the trails at a slower speed, but none less exciting, until we reach his truck. He loads his ATV back up in the bed of his truck, and then walks over to me.

"Get naked," he orders with a wave of his brow.

I look around, seeing nothing but trees and sky, and then because I'm too busy wondering about his list and bucket riddles, I pull my mud soaked shirt over my head. His eyes shoot straight to my chest and I smirk to myself when he groans.

"Towel," he barks after I wrestle my wet jeans down. He wraps a clean towel around my body, then folds at the knees to help me step out of my pants. "Leave your panties on. I know it isn't comfortable with the mud and all, but if you take them off I wouldn't even care if it was a dirty fuck, I would take you so hard."

"Ohhh kay, so they stay on," I sarcastically draw out.

"While I get ready. Pull the glove box open and grab my list. Mark off number three, and then take a look. Pick which ones you want to experience together, then cross off the ones you don't. Then our list becomes a bucket."

"Do you mean bucket list? What? Did you have one before? I don't think they work like that, Lee. You can't take your bucket list for yourself and make it a couples project."

He doesn't respond; too busy peeling his mud-soaked clothes off before wrapping a towel around his hips. I roll my eyes and move to climb into his truck, pressing the latch on his glove box and reaching in to grab the solo piece of paper on top of his owner's manual.

I recognize the handwriting as Dani's and my brow pulls tight. I do a quick scan to see it's a good size list, full of activates. On the top, Feeling Alive, is written boldly and underlined. Two items already crossed off, reading them both brings tears instantly to my eyes. Paintball and Karaoke. It hits me then that this isn't *his* bucket list, it's the one he created as mine. Or better yet, going by the title, he created this as a map for his plan. My hand shakes when I see the third line has "muddin'" written in Dani's neat script.

"I had this brilliant plan that if I did enough things that made you feel, it'd cause your body to spike in adrenaline and your heart to go out of control, that you would remember how much fun being alive is. You'd been living in a dark place and I just knew you were keeping yourself from feeling in order to protect yourself. I understood it, darlin', every bit of it, but in order to make you see how much I care, I had to remind you that feeling alive is worth the fight."

"Oh, God," I mutter.

"I figured I could have stopped the list when you became mine, but then I remembered how beautiful it is to see you experiencing the beauty of living. So, instead of Feeling Alive, we make a new list, Feeling Together. You pick from there, or we pick together, but we make a list of things to do. Once a month, Molly goes to Mom's and we live our lives, together, and never stop feeling."

I look back at the list, smiling when I see 'sex' made the list at number ten. My voice coming unstuck and I look back at

Lee. He's studying my reaction and I notice, to my shock, that he seems nervous.

"Sex wasn't until number ten?" I ask and his shoulders relax and his dimple comes out.

"Well, yes and no. I didn't tell Dani when she helped me write that list, but *that* sex was public sex and not just sex, sex. I hadn't planned it out yet, but I figured that one could move around when we found a bathroom with a sturdy lock on it."

I laugh, place the list down in my lap and reach out to grab his hand.

"Could we maybe add some things that Molly can do with us?" I ask.

"Yeah, darlin', I would love that."

"Then as far as I can tell, we've got a good list to keep us busy for a while. But, Lee . . . there is no way in hell you're going to get my to jump out of a plane or off a bridge. No way."

He throws his head back and roars with laughter. My hand tightens on his and I watch as his abs flex with his rumbles and when his eyes meet mine again there is nothing but love in them.

"You're going to enjoy every step of us feeling together, darlin'," he vows.

"I already do, Liam. I already do."

Chapter 28

Megan

"OH, GOD!" I SCREAM WHEN Lee tightens his hold on my hips and pulls my body back forcefully to meet his thrusting hips. When he pulls back just a breath and then slams back inside my body, I clamp down.

"So tight. Fuck, the way you squeeze my cock, darlin'." His voice is strained and when he pulls back, my pussy clamps tight in response, not wanting him to leave me.

"Please, Lee," I beg with no idea of what I need except for him to make it happen.

"Fuck," he growls and his hands leave my hips when he pulls completely from my body, causing me to whine instantly, before I'm flipped and his body is covering mine.

"You'll get my cock, Megan. Fuck, when you make that noise I swear to Christ I can feel it in my balls. Pulling tight until I have no doubt I could come from you making that sexy as fuck whine from losing my cock."

Instantly, I mewl and whine, the sound making him close his eyes.

My hips rock against his and I watch as his jaw clenches, making those sexy flexes pop out near his ear. Of course, since I find that ridiculously hot, my hips pick up speed and his cock, already wet with my excitement, slides between my folds. He doesn't open his eyes, but his hands come and frame my face, his palms holding my head by my ears and his long fingers curling around the top of my head.

"Come inside me, baby," I beg, wanting him to fill me so badly that I'm panting for it.

His eyes hold mine and he groans when, again, I rock my hips. "I love you, Megan."

My heart thumps, "I love you, Lee."

His hips move this time, slowly. "So much, darlin'," he murmurs and then closes his eyes.

"Yes," I breathe. "So much."

He pulls back his hips, but doesn't move the rest of his body, keeping us connected from hips to head when his lips brush lightly over mine.

"You've given me the world," he says, still whispering.

I nod and then gasp when he moves his hips back in, my legs coming up, and his cock filling me without aide.

"I'll love you until I take my last breath," he pants, his hips thrusting in a torturously slow speed. "Forever, Megan."

"Yes. God, yes, Lee. Forever."

His eyes never leave mine. His thrusts never speed up. When we both come, together, I watch as one small tear leaks out of his eye and falls onto my face. He doesn't speak or acknowledge the sign of how deep his love is rooted that still burns an invisible trail down until his tear is lost in my hair. When we both come down from our climb, he doesn't leave my body, just wraps his arms tighter and pulls us to his side.

We fall asleep like that and while in the safety of his arms I feel the peace I've been working for. All the pain of the past vanishing as I let go of the last hold it had on me and while I drift off to sleep, thank God that Lee brought me back to life.

Liam

I felt it.

When she finally let go and gave me all of her.

It was a moment that rocked me straight to my core.

When she gave me her body, I watched that last tiny bit of fear bleed from her face, and the realization that she can trust in our love enough to let go.

I don't know what I did in my life to deserve her love but whatever it was I'll spend the rest of my life making sure I'm worthy of that gift.

Her body goes slack and I know she's asleep, but I still can't get my arms to let go. I hold on, all through the night, and not once do my arms slip.

"Darlin'," I call down the hall, grabbing my keys off the table by the door before walking down the hall, "Megan?"

"In here," she grumbles from the closet.

"What the hell?" I question when I walk into her room. "Did your closet throw up?"

"Funny." She moves back from her closet and almost trips on the shoes that are scattered on the floor. "I was looking for my black boots, but I think they've vanished to the same mysterious land that my socks always go missing to."

"Mysterious land?"

Her hands come up and plant on her hips. "I'll have you know that place is real. How else do you explain how hundreds of socks a year just vanish? Poof. Gone and never to be seen again."

"My guess? They probably just fall behind or under the dryer."

Her eyes narrow.

"Or maybe they vanish to a mysterious land," I add with a smile.

Her eyes soften and she smirks. "Okay, so I'll admit that maybe I'm losing my mind because I have to finish this book and I know that, I do, but I can't seem to figure out how to end it. It's like the ending is right there, and I know it's going to be so beautiful, I just can't find the right words."

I reach out and lightly tug at her biceps until she shuffles forward, wrapping her arms around my waist and dropping her forehead against my chest.

"It's right there, Lee."

I fold her in my arms and bend to kiss the top of her head. "Maybe, darlin', you can't find the words because the story isn't finished."

Her head tips up and rests against my chest with her chin. "Meaning?"

"I'm not going to pretend to understand what goes on in your head when you're writing those brilliant books of yours, but baby, you've told me enough about this book that I see all the parallels with our own story. Maybe you can't find the end because it's not ready to be written."

Her nose crinkles and she bites her lip.

"I love you, darlin'. Take the time you need to work it out. I'll go pick up Molly from Mom and we'll go out to lunch. That should give you a few hours to figure out what you need."

"Okay, I can do that," she says, but I can tell she isn't paying attention. I've already lost her to her words.

I love watching her work. I could have a full conversation with her and she wouldn't hear a word of it because her mind is still playing chess with her characters.

I also wasn't kidding when I told her why I think she's held up on ending her newest book. She's let me read the beginning of *The Helping Hand,* a book she told me was titled after me. Or better yet, my urging in the beginning of our relationship to take my hand. It wasn't a shock after hearing that that the book she's working on might as well be a biography of her life.

Which is exactly why I think she can't finish it.

Yet.

But that should all change soon.

As long as my lunch date with my favorite five-year-old goes as planned, that is.

"I'll be home later," I tell her and kiss her forehead again.

"Buckle up, little lady," I tell Molly before shutting the door of my truck and turning back to my mom.

"She's a sweetheart, Liam."

"I know, Mom. Best girl in the world," I tell her, making her smile grow.

"I'm guessing you already know this, if I'm judging your plans today correctly, but you don't have to worry. That little girl already thinks the world of you."

I close my eyes and nod.

"In fact, I think you'll be happy with what you find out if you just ask her."

"Ask her what, Mom?"

"To be her daddy," she leans forward and whispers, looking behind me where Molly is singing along to the radio.

"She's already got a daddy, Mom. I would love to hear those words from her one day, but I don't want to take her father's place. I'd gladly share the role, but not take it when it's already been taken. God, I'm a nervous mess."

She reaches forward and pats my cheek, "I know you are. It's a big step, but one I know you're ready for. I've told you over and over how much of your father I see in you, but watching you fall in love with Megan really brought that home. Don't second guess yourself, son. I understand what you're saying about Molly and her daddy, but just because she has a father that she lost, doesn't mean you would be replacing him by stepping into those shoes. That girl has more love to give then she could ever figure out how to give out."

"As far as I'm concerned she's already my daughter."

My mother's wise eyes look into mine and she smiles, "And as far as your father and I are concerned she's already our grand-daughter, so . . . I suspect it's up to you to make that official."

I laugh, say my goodbye and then hug my mom before jumping into the driver's seat.

"You and me have a date today," I tell a smiling Molly.

Her eyes grow huge and she looks over at me like I hold all the secrets in the world. "A date?"

"Yeah. You're my favorite little girl in the whole entire universe. It's time for me to show you off. Let everyone know that you're mine."

Her eyes don't lose their wide wonderment, but she gives me a small grin. "I'm yours?" she questions.

"Forever and ever, stuck with the biggest, stickiest, gooiest piece of bubblegum in the whole world."

She laughs, loud, and smiles at me with her crooked smile.

Molly chatters off and on about everything she did at my parent's house the night before. I don't hear much, my nerves too busy holding my attention, but I slip in responses here and there, each time her big smile grows a little more.

God, I love that kid.

When we get to the Italian restaurant that she loves so much, I make a big production of walking around to her side of the truck, pulling the back door of the duel cab open, and offering her my arm after helping her climb down. The whole time she just giggles.

Her snickers don't stop until we've placed our order and our drinks are delivered.

"Leelee?"

"Yes, sweetheart?"

"I love you more than the moon," she says softly with an undertone of unsureness that has me moving from the seat in front of her, to the one next to her.

"Molly, look at me baby," I demand and wait for her to move her light brown eyes from her water. "You want to know a secret?"

Her small head nods and she continues to study my face.

"I had another reason, other than showing the prettiest five-year-old in the whole universe off, to take you out on a date, just me and you. You see, I have big huge plans that I need to make with you. Plans I need to be kept a super-secret, secret. Can you do that?"

She gives me another nod, a small smile coming over her face, and I can tell she's losing some of that uncertainty that had come when telling me that she loved me. This little girl, having gone through so much in her little life, who loves bigger than anyone I know, is actually afraid I would turn her love away.

"You need to know, without a single doubt that I love you

back, sweetheart. I love you just as much as I love your mommy, and that, Molly, is huge."

"How huge?" she whispers.

"All the way to the sun. All the way to the moon. All the way to the farthest star away from us. And then back again."

"That's really, really far away," she gasps.

"It sure is. I told you. I love you huge, sweetheart."

She's silent for a few seconds and I sit back. When her small hand reaches out and lands on the one I have resting just besides her water glass, I look back up and see questions in her eyes.

"What's on your mind, Molly?"

"If you love me huge and I love you huge, does that mean that you'll be my second daddy now?"

And my heart, when I didn't think it could get any bigger, grows so large my chest burns with it.

"There isn't anything I would love more, Molly."

"Yay," she says, her tone soft and her eyes bright.

"Yay," I answer in my own hushed tone.

"One more thing, baby, and then we can have the best spaghetti in town. Are you ready for that big, huge secret? You can't tell anyone."

Her head bobs, each long blonde ringlet dancing against her skin.

"In a few days, I'm going to take your mommy somewhere, somewhere special to us because the last time we were there she took my hand and never let it go. This time, sweetheart, this time I'm hoping that she takes my hand again. The only difference is, when she takes it this time, it means the three of us become a family."

"That sounds fun, Le—Daddy," she whispers.

And there goes that sharpness in my chest. Again.

"I have to ask you something first though, Molly. Something that's a huge secret so you can't tell your mommy, but I have to ask *you* because in order to have your mommy give me her hand, I want to know you will too."

She pats my hand and laughs. "I already gave you my hand, silly."

I smile and nod. "You sure have, sweetheart. But what I mean is, I'm going to ask your mommy for her hand so that I can give her a ring. A beautiful ring that only queens and princesses get. And if she tells me yes, I get to take her hand and put that big beautiful ring on there. That way everyone knows that your mommy took my hand forever and ever."

I reach down into my jeans and pull out a bracelet that I had picked up last weekend. It's a simple silver bracelet with one charm hanging on it. The charm is a single teapot with a base made of three diamonds. One for her, one for her mom and one, for me.

"I don't have a ring for you, little lady, but I do have this. I want to give you this so that everyone knows that you gave me your hand forever and ever. I put a teapot on there so you will always remember how much fun we have when we have our tea parties."

Her eyes move from the charm, to my face and back to the charm. Her little chin wobbles and for a second I fear that I've made a mistake. Maybe she isn't ready for this.

Those thoughts vanish instantly when she jumps from her seat and throws her arms around my neck. I lose sight of the table when her curls hit me in the face and my arms go around her tiny body.

"You're going to be the bestest second daddy in the whole entire world," she whispers in my ear.

Chapter 29

Liam

I HAVE NO CLUE HOW MOLLY has kept our secret this long, but one week turned in to two, and then two went into three. Before I knew it, work had kept me from executing my plan for a month. Somehow I had gotten roped into working every weekend for the last four straight. When Barnes, one of the other HTPD officers, asked me to work tonight for him, I gave him not just a no, but a hell no.

With our schedules being as crazy as they are, by the time I would get to Megan's, Molly would either be going to bed, or already asleep. What little time I've had with her, has been rushed.

I had been hesitant to start spending the night more than every once in a while, but it wasn't Megan who had put an end to my reluctance. Two weeks ago, it was Molly.

"Never leave us, Daddy! Never, never, never, ever! Please

don't go. Stop going. We need you." Molly sobbed against my chest, where she had launched herself when I tried to leave the house two weeks ago.

Megan gasped, her hand going to her mouth and her eyes filling with tears. She had heard Molly call me Daddy a few times, but they had been infrequent as if she was testing the waters. There was nothing unsure about the way it came out of her mouth this time. Unable to do anything else with a small human attached to my body like she was trying to fuse herself to me, I sat back down on the couch I had just climbed up from and wrapped her in my arms.

It was very rare for Molly to have any sort of temper tantrums. Even more unusual for her to cry. I've only seen her cry a handful of times. She fell off her bike a month ago and tore her knees to shreds, not one tear. But what's coming from her right now is rivers of tears.

"Sweetheart, what's going on?" I ask and rub her small back, willing her to calm down.

"You can't leave us. Please don't go. We want you forever," she pleads.

Hearing her little voice while it begs me to never let go, killed. I look over to Megan to see her shake her head, her eyes red with the strength she's putting out just to keep her tears locked tight.

"Molly, look at me, honey," I request, feeling her body shake with sobs. "Baby, look at me."

Her head comes up, brown eyes red rimmed and her nose and cheeks reddened. I reach over, grab a tissue off the side table next to the couch, and help her dry her face. She sniffles a few times and I give her what I hope is a reassuring smile.

"I'm not going anywhere, baby. I was just going to go back to my house tonight. I wasn't leaving you. I'll never leave you."

"Wh . . . why can't you stay?" she demands, her voice shaking with the sadness leftover. "Why can't you just live here?"

I look back up to Megan, waiting for her help guiding this conversation. With a nod, she sits down next to us, taking my hand in one of hers and placing the other against Molly's back.

"Little bird, it isn't that he doesn't want to stay with us, that's just a big step that when adults decide to make it, they talk about it first."

Molly's eyes look between the two of us a few times and then with all the wisdom of a small child says, "Then talk about it."

"Uh," Megan stutters.

"Mommy, do you want Daddy to live with us forever and ever and always?" she asks, Megan, her small voice strong and sure.

Megan looks at me, her eyes wide, and I watch as she has a million emotions filter across her face, until finally settling on love.

"Yeah, little bird, I would love it."

Molly looks from her mom over to me and smiles a little bigger.

"Daddy, do you want to live with your girls forever and ever and always?"

With nothing left but to accept that a five-year-old has just put two adults in their place, I tighten my hold on Molly, reach out and pull Megan into our embrace and after moving my head close, I tell her without a shadow of doubt, "Yes, baby. I would love nothing more."

We waited until Molly had gone to bed that night before we finished the conversation. In the end, I moved what I needed and settled into their home. We both decided that selling the only house that Molly has known was a step that would come later, for now, all three of us wanted to be together and together we were.

Now, a month later from when I had originally planned it, I was coming off a shift and meeting Megan with the rest of our friends at Mike's.

After folding my body into the truck, I was about to call Megan when my phone rang.

"Hey, darlin'," I answered.

"Hey you. We're at Mike's now. Are you on the way?"

"Just left the station. Did Molly do okay tonight when you left her?"

Megan laughs, "Yes, honey. Her fever is gone and she's jumping around all over the place. I told you the doctor said it was just a little virus and it would run its course."

"That was five days ago," I complain. "Five days of her running a fever doesn't make me happy."

Megan lets out a small laugh, "You'll get used to it, Lee. She's a kid. They sometimes get sick like that."

"Doesn't mean I have to like it."

"All right. Let's take the over-protective mode down a few degrees. She's fine and need I remind you that she's with your parents? Parents that have raised a son perfectly, I might add."

"My mom let me wear her heels, baby. I'm not sure we can

say perfectly."

Megan laughs and I hear the noise of Mike's start getting louder.

"You going in now?" I ask.

"Yeah, I think everyone else is here. Cohen and Dani are waiting by the door for me."

My chest swells when I think about all of our friends being there for this. It wasn't hard, talking everyone in to my plans. Hell, they didn't need a bit of urging. When I mentioned the ring, the girls would never have been able to stay away. The guys don't care about that like the girls, but I know my friends are just happy that Megan and I have found this together.

"Right, darlin'. Go inside and grab a drink. I'll be there soon."

I get her sweet voice telling me she loves me and any nerves that I had earlier evaporated instantly.

It's time to go get the girl.

The bar is crowded when I walk in. I look over to our usual corner and see that Dani had followed through, making sure that Megan was in the chair with her back to the stage. Nate and Cohen see me the second I walk in, clearly being tasked with lookout duty. I watch as dumb and dumber smile huge. Cohen knocks his knee over and it hits Dani, who snaps her head up and looks toward the door. Her eyes connect with mine and I watch as they start to get misty.

Jesus, that girl.

Nate coughs so loud that I can hear him across the room and over the music. I shake my head at his obvious move to clue the rest of our friends in that I've arrived. Lyn and Lila make a slow circle, looking around the room until they see me. I get a wink from both of them, which always freaks me out when they do twin things. Stella stands and stretches, looking behind her and I get a smile before she turns back toward the group and drops back down on the couch next to the twins.

Maddi and her sister, Ember, are less obvious. They're facing me on the other couch and they don't react, just give me their eyes as both of them tip their lips up slightly.

The only one that doesn't move or react is Zac, but with him sitting next to Megan, there isn't a way he could do that without her catching on. But I see his hand come out and rest on the back of Megan's chair. She laughs as he continues whatever they've been talking about and without missing a beat, his thumb comes up on the hand resting behind her.

With a light step, I make my way over to the side of the stage and wait for my turn. I called ahead, so they know what's going on, but because I got held up at work I wasn't there right on time.

I nod at Bennett, the guy in charge of handling the karaoke end of Mike's, and let him know I'm ready when he is. I wait as two drunken idiots butcher *Friends in Low Places* and then it's my turn. Bennett doesn't announce me, or the song, he just hands the mic over and starts up the only song I requested.

The first cords of Train's *Marry Me* fill the room and I walk to the center of the stage, not feeling a lick of my stage fright as I clear my throat and open my mouth.

My eyes don't leave Megan's back, so I don't miss her jolting when I sing the first line. She doesn't turn until I start the chorus. The second those two words are out of my mouth, I watch Zac snag her glass right before it goes crashing to the ground.

Then I move.

I jump off the stage and ignore the crowded bar full of people screaming and cheering. I only have eyes for the beautiful blonde staring at me with huge tears rolling down her face. I take the long path, going around all the tables before I even get close to her. I give everything I have while singing that song to her. Smile on my face and a love so strong for this woman that I feel the emotion of this moment filling my body.

My feet take me to her and I reach out to grab her hand before I drop to my knee. Singing the last word out clearly until the last note in the song plays.

"Well, darlin'? Make me the happiest man in the whole world. Marry me and give *me* everything this time?"

She nods, her head bobbing swiftly and her tears picking up speed.

"God, yes!" she screams.

I reach my hand out, not caring who takes it, passing off the mic. Before I move from the floor, I grab the ring that had been burning a hole in my pocket, and slip it onto her waiting hand.

Then I grab my woman, ignoring the catcalls that follow as I place an arm under her knees and another around her waist until I have her in my arms. She throws her head back, laughing through her tears and I carry her out the door.

To our future.

Epilogue

Megan

"**HEY**," I WHISPER INTO THE wind. "It's a beautiful day. You would hate it though. We had a cold front come in last week and it's been so amazingly cold."

Silence greets me. It always does, but it doesn't hurt anymore.

"I miss you," I sigh, leaning forward and dusting some of the dead leaves off the headstone. "Molly has her first boyfriend. Well, she says boyfriend, but they're eight. Lee's having a hard time with that, but you would love how protective he is of her. He actually asked me if he could lock her up." I laugh, thinking about how adamant he had been about his grand plan of keeping his girl from any boys. "Anyway, she talked him down from that. I swear that girl could talk him into anything."

The wind picks up and I pull my coat a little tighter against

Bleeding LOVE

my body before adjusting my scarf.

"She's growing so fast, Jack. I look at her and I see so much of myself. You used to always say that. Even when she was a tiny baby you would pick out parts of her that were all me. But she acts like you. Sees beauty in everything. So full of happiness, that girl. I'm glad. I know that in my heart, regardless of the truth, that she got that from her father—you."

I watch some leaves fall from the huge trees that surround the area around me. Each one twirling and swirling on the way to the ground before settling.

"Jack will be six months this weekend. He's such a good baby. And Molly is loving that her baby brother is finally big enough, mobile enough, that she can play with him more."

Looking back at the headstone, I smile, and start to climb from my kneeling position, careful of my slightly rounded stomach.

"Of course, it's harder for me now with another one on the way. We haven't found out the sex yet, but something tells me I've got another boy coming. Lee thinks you've played a part in making sure I have a little army surrounding me. I've got to say, he's probably not wrong."

I look around once more, seeing the fall weather settling around us and before I tell him goodbye, I look over at Lee leaning against our SUV waiting patiently with his long legs crossed at the ankles and his back against the door, while I have my chat with Jack.

"I haven't told you in a while, but thank you. For everything you did to make sure that Molly and I were safe. For getting us out and bringing us to Hope Town. I wish you were still with us, but even in passing you set us up for a future of everything bright. I'm so happy, Jack. Not a day goes by that I don't miss you, but Lee has brought something so special into our lives and I know somewhere you're resting easy knowing that."

The wind picks up and I turn my head when I hear heavy footsteps fall in behind me. Lee gives me his knee-melting smile that hasn't gotten any less brilliant in three years.

"You ready?" he questions.

"Always, Lee."

Lee turns his head and glances at Jack's headstone. He doesn't speak, but every time we come out here he takes a few seconds to just look.

"Are *you* ready?" I ask, smiling up at my husband.

His arm goes around my waist and I feel his hand over my pregnant stomach.

"Always. Just telling Jack thanks for handing me the world again."

His head dips and I get a soft kiss before we turn and walk toward the SUV. Lee's hand moves from my waist and his warm fingers close around my hand.

"I love you, darlin'," he tells me his eyes full of love and his dimple flashing.

"I love you back."

Feeling Alive

1. Paintball
2. Karaoke
3. 4-Wheeling
4. Six Flags (roller coasters)
5. Bungee Jumping (really, Lee?)
6. Sky Diving (Ha! Good luck with that)
7. Zip lining
8. Tattoo (a little overkill, I think)
9. White Water Rafting
10. Sex ;)
11. Rock Concert
12. Playing in the rain
13. Surfing
14. Rock Climbing
15. Swim with dolphins
16. Road trip to anywhere
17. Making her fall in love (Had to)

Acknowledgments

After 8 books this part gets harder and harder. To every single person that helped me build this book from the ground up. My brilliant editors, Ellie and Emma, for making sure I don't look like an idiot. My extremely talented cover designer Sommer for knowing each time exactly what is in my head. Brilliant gifted eye behind the lens, Lauren. My models, Taylor and Laura, you guys . . . seriously, thank you for bringing Liam and Megan to life. My formatter, Stacey, whom I love, for always making my pages beautiful . . . putting up with my insanity. The ladies at The Rock Stars of Romance for hosting my tour and release blitz. You guys always take such good care of my 'babies' and me. Each and every member of my Alpha Babes group. You guys keep me going, help me when I need it, and never fail to let me know how much you love these characters.

To my amazing, incredible, kickass readers. Your love for not only me, but also my characters, fuels my soul like you would never believe. When I need my own 'helping hand' you never let me down. I can't even tell you all how much each and every one of you mean to me. Thank YOU, for always believing in me. Thank YOU, for opening your hearts and letting my characters feel YOUR love.

To my family . . . you guys deal with me at my worst and my best. You put up with my insanity and my (somewhat) sanity. I am who I am because of you. And my girls, M, T, and A . . . you make mommy want to be the best she can be. You push me to dig deep and never give up. But, you still can never read my books.

And to Felicia Lynn. You're crazy, but a good crazy. Not the kind of crazy that makes me worried you know my alarm code, but the kind that makes me fucking thrilled to call you my BFF. You don't judge me silently, or behind my back, but you tell me to my face how insane I am. That, and that there is no one I know that I could sit next to for hours a day and say so much without speaking one word. You get me. Wait for it . . . but I still won't fucking cuddle you, you weirdo.